A Texas Family Time Capsule

Ruth Pennebaker

Republic of Texas Press
Plano, Texas

Library of Congress Cataloging-in-Publication Data

Pennebaker, Ruth
A Texas family time capsule / Ruth Pennebaker.
    p. cm.
Most of the essays appeared originally in the Dallas Morning News'
Viewpoints, Today, and Texas living sections; some appeared in the New
York Times, American way, Redbook, and Special reports-Family.
ISBN 1-55622-894-5
I. Title.
PN4874.P433 A25   2002
814'.54—dc21   2002000462
                                                       CIP

Republic of Texas Press is an imprint of Wordware Publishing, Inc.
No part of this book may be reproduced in any form or by
any means without permission in writing from
Wordware Publishing, Inc.

Printed in the United States of America

ISBN 1-55622-894-5
10 9 8 7 6 5 4 3 2 1
0201

All inquiries for volume purchases of this book should be addressed to
Wordware Publishing, Inc., at 2320 Los Rios Boulevard, Plano, Texas
75074. Telephone inquiries may be made by calling:

(972) 423-0090

For my father, Hiram S. Burney, who always
photocopied my columns

Contents

Contents

Contents

Author's Note

Most of these essays appeared originally in the *Dallas Morning News'* Viewpoints, Today, and Texas Living sections. A few others appeared in *The New York Times*, *American Way*, *Redbook*, and *Special Reports—Family*.

Acknowledgments

Thanks to my wonderful agent, Lois Wallace, and to my family for putting up with me (and for giving me credit for not writing about some of the best stories—since I can be, upon occasion, a discreet person).

Introduction

What should she do in the middle of a crisis? a woman asks
her mother in Nora Ephron's novel Heartburn.
"Take notes," her mother advises.

I can relate to that. Even when I'm not in the middle of a crisis, I still take notes.

I've spent the past several years writing mostly about family life. When I began our daughter was seven, our son was three, and my husband and I were barely in our forties. It was the last decade of the last century of the millennium, but I don't think we gave it much thought at the time. We were too busy with work and family life and friends, trying to stay semi-sane, trying to stay afloat.

In the headlines of the past several years, the stock market soared, the presidency was embroiled in scandal, countries were split and bloodied by war, the earth warmed alarmingly, and high technology swiftly invaded our lives. But it was the smaller stories, the ones closer to home, that always captivated me. Home life was—what? Simpler? No. More easily understandable? Uh-uh. Safer? No way. (You know how you always read that the home is the most dangerous place for injuries and accidents? Well, that's not even talking about the hazards of loving other people and trying to live with them. Some things you can't reduce to statistics.)

But that's what has always intrigued me—human emotions, how we live together, how we love each other and fail each other and drive each other nuts, the small moments that can pass before we realize how significant they were. To me, there's nothing more complex or important.

So I took notes over the past several years, through the orthodontia, the music lessons, the squabbles, the housework that doesn't get done, the cats, the hormones, the daily brouhaha, the carpools, the lice. When the crises came—the deaths of parents and close friends, a parent's diagnosis with Alzheimer's disease, when one of us got cancer and both of us went bald—I went on taking notes and writing. It's a hard habit to break.

By now our daughter has begun college and our son is in high school, and the years look better on them than they do on my husband and me. What would I call the two of us? I don't know. Maybe battered but exhilarated. We've been through years that were tragic and funny and everything in between. But I have the tendency to find life amusing much of the time and screamingly hilarious at other points—when it's not driving me crazy or breaking my heart. I can't help it. It's like an itch I have to scratch.

Over these years I've been fortunate enough to be able to write about what I think and feel, my observations, my pet peeves (e.g., movies co-starring ancient leading men and fresh-faced ingénues; badly written, photocopied Christmas brag sheets; militant vegetarians, the IRS, and Martha Stewart), what's important to me, what's happened to me, what hasn't happened but might. It's a strange life, when I think about it. On those days when the skies open up and the roof leaks, when the cat hurls herself out of a tree and breaks her leg, when somebody throws up when I'm driving a carpool, when my stockings run, and the fire department investigates my husband's pyromaniacal leanings, I can shriek and swear and cry. But I also know that the worse the day, the better the column.

At other times, when I look around and don't notice anything that interests me, I write a column where I make the whole thing up. Which is where you can find in these pages a new frequent-flier program for airlines that rewards the spouse who stays at home (an idea too far ahead of its time, evidently, owing to narrow and linear thinking on the industry's part), a job advice column by Monica Lewinsky, and a "scientific" Valentine's Day report about how the sight of men doing housework is an aphrodisiac for women.

So that's what this book of columns is. It doesn't lend itself to neat, clear-cut description. It's mostly the story of a fairly good-natured, often good-humored Texas family skidding and lurching into the new millennium. It's about cultural trends as seen by a non-trendy person. It's about the small moments in life and the large moments and how you find life on what you'd thought was the sidelines.

I don't know. Maybe it's the story of why people take notes about their lives. It's so you can look back, years later, and finally understand what you were writing about and how and why you were living.

— Ruth Pennebaker

Chapter 1

In a Family Way

Goodbye, Dr. Spock

Name a book on childrearing. Any book. By the time I had two children, I'd read them all. Books on disciplining your children. Accepting them. Understanding them. Raising them, rearing them, hearing them—

"I hate Nicholas," our daughter announced one day. "He's funny-looking."

Teal was four then, and her younger brother was a newborn. We weren't having one of our better days. The temperature had skidded to 90, our house was on the market, and my husband was in Sweden. I was expecting a migraine any minute.

"I don't know *why* people think Nicky's so cute," she continued.

Aha. Sibling rivalry. Right on schedule, according to the stack of books I'd read. *Your child is understandably concerned about a new baby. It's a good sign when he or she verbalizes his or her hostility. Ask him or her to talk more about it.*

"You sound as if you're angry at Nicholas," I said, using my best "active-listening" voice. I picked up Nicholas, who had started to scream.

Teal, in turn, actively ignored my active listening.

"You know," she said ominously, "a lot of little babies are kidnapped. Nicky may get kidnapped someday. But that would be fine. Then we could have a sister named Elizabeth." She looked quite happy at the prospect.

Encourage your child to let out his or her emotions when—

The phone rang. It was our realtor, calling to announce she would be showing our house in 45 minutes. "Just tidy up the house a little," she advised.

I hung up and put Nicholas in his infant seat. Then I looked around. Big mistake. The kitchen was a disaster—dishes overflowing in the sink, a major oatmeal spill, and toys everywhere. Teal was on the floor, using a felt marker to color her Barbie doll's hair green.

"We're going to clean up the house a little," I said to her. I used my "reasonable" voice. *Reason with a child and he or she will surprise you by being reasonable him- or herself.* "Will you please pick up your Barbie doll and Magic Markers and put them away?"

"No way," Teal said. "I'm not in the mood."

Ignore negativism. Be pleasant and focus on the positive. "Neither am I," I said in my nicest voice. "But we've got to clean up, anyway. Will you please put up your Barbie doll and markers now?"

"I'm not a maid," Teal said.

When your child refuses to do something, this is a sign that he or she knows his or her own mind. You wouldn't really want a passive child who said yes to everything, would you? Frankly, that sounds rather attractive, I thought.

"You will clean up now because I told you so," I said, my voice rising.

"You're being rude!" Teal shouted. "And you're yelling at me!"

When your child argues with you, it shows that he or she isn't afraid of you. Isn't that wonderful?

Hell, no, I thought. What's wrong with a little judicious fear now and then?

"You will clean up in here—or I'll give you a spanking," I said. Teal suddenly became very industrious.

A parent who threatens physical punishment has failed. And a parent who listens to too many experts on child discipline will go nuts, I thought. Why not listen to yourself occasionally? After all, *You know more than you think you do.*

I grinned. Actually, I couldn't have said it better myself.

Trophy Children

You want trophies? My children have lots of trophies. They also have medals and rainbows of blue, red, white, and pink ribbons. Look at their walls and you'll see certificates of merit, certificates for perfect attendance, certificates for good citizenship.

I would say their bedrooms are like shrines or something, but I don't think they make shrines this messy. Woody Allen must have been right when he said that 80 percent of success is just showing up, because these days, they even give you a trophy for it.

I know, I know. All these awards and trophies and ribbons are supposed to give our children high self-esteem. If we praise our children and reward them, the rationale goes, they'll be stronger and better suited to tackle the world.

The trouble is, I'm sick of hearing about self-esteem, and this constant stream of awards and chirpy praise is beginning to give me cluster headaches. I want my children to be confident and to think well of themselves. But I'm not sure this is the way to go about it.

We're trying to give our children too much, too easily. Hand them big trophies for a fourth-place finish and all you're doing is whetting their appetites for bigger trophies if they ever finish third. This isn't the road to self-esteem; it's the road to trophy- and ego-inflation.

Who knows? Like everything else with children, you roll the dice and make decisions—and twenty years down the line, you find out whether you were right or wrong or *non compos mentis*. Maybe we'll find we've reared a generation of children who are strong and self-assured and have lots of trophies. Or maybe we'll find we've brought up children who have false expectations about a world where there isn't enough love and good fortune and praise to go around.

With all our emphasis on self-esteem, though, I don't think we're teaching our children to think more *of* themselves. We're teaching them to think more *about* themselves.

To me, giving or pursuing self-esteem is as elusive as giving or pursuing happiness. I'm not sure you can stake it out and claim it for yourself or anyone else. You don't feel happy because you're trying to feel happy; you feel happy when you've forgotten to ask yourself every fifteen seconds whether you're happy or not. You feel happy when you've forgotten yourself.

What I think we can give our children—or teach them—is the joy of losing themselves in something bigger, of immersing themselves, of losing their self-absorption, of earning their own rewards. I realize that sounds suspiciously like work. I realize, too, that it also sounds neurotic and competitive and driven and all those other things you're not supposed to want to pass on to your children these days.

But I'd rather see my own children striving after something and working for it and enjoying the pursuit. I'd rather see that any day than to see them sitting in a corner, complacent and self-satisfied and expecting to get an award for breathing well.

"I always worried about Jennifer's self-esteem," one of my friends told me about her daughter. "She made C's, and I knew she could make B's if she worked harder, but it didn't bother her. She has high self-esteem even though she's making C's, and I guess that's what I wanted. She's very pleased with herself."

Pleased with herself, no matter what?

Two or three years ago, my husband was scolding our daughter about something she'd done wrong. After she listened to him, she said, "When you tell me that, I don't feel good about myself."

Exactly, darlin', I thought. At this point, there's no reason why you should.

———— 🍎 ————

Why Henry the Duck Moved On

For years my husband and I read to our children every night. We were teaching them to love books and helping them learn values.

The idea was great, but the reality was more like a battle of wills. The minute our children learned to talk, they developed very strong opinions about the books they wanted to hear.

"Read Rainbow Brite!" our three-year-old daughter commanded night after night.

I hated Rainbow Brite. She had vacant-looking blue eyes and a bright yellow ponytail. She also had about as much personality as a celery stalk, but she wasn't nearly as smart.

"Why do you like Rainbow Brite so much?" I'd ask casually.

"Because she's so pretty," our daughter would say.

Great. Just wonderful. I was a washout as a feminist role model. I was reading our daughter a book that taught her the importance of being pretty. At least Rainbow Brite looked a little plump, though. As far as I could tell, she wasn't anorexic or anything.

The years passed, and our daughter outgrew Rainbow Brite. One summer afternoon we finally sold Rainbow and all her books at a garage sale. She left with another family and she never looked back.

But the bedtime-reading battles raged on. My husband was convinced that our son had developed an unhealthy fixation with the Berenstain Bears. He made the Bears sound even worse than Rainbow Brite. "They're completely lacking in charm and a sense of humor," he grumbled.

My husband, who considers neatness a character flaw, especially disliked *The Berenstain Bears and the Messy Room*—the story of how Brother and Sister Bear learned how much fun it was to have a clean house. He always read the book in what I considered a very subversive way.

"Don't you think Brother and Sister Bear are a little obsessive-compulsive?" I'd hear him ask our son. "Do you *really* think that being neat and clean is that much fun?" he'd ask in a doubtful voice.

Some nights my husband would insist on equal time for a book he really liked, *Henry's Awful Mistake*. It was the story of Henry the Duck, who was preparing dinner for his friend Clara when he noticed an ant in his kitchen. Henry became very upset and tried to kill the ant—and ended up breaking his water pipes, flooding his house, and getting washed out into the street. My husband called this a morality tale. "Look what happens when you obsess about minor details in life," he told our son.

Later, Henry moves to a new house, where he prepares dinner for Clara once again. He sees another ant and recalls his painful lesson. "He looked the other way!" the book ends, cheerfully.

"Look the other way!" my husband always chortled. "I love that! Look the other way!"

"That *is* pretty funny," our son agreed. He started to request *Henry's Awful Mistake* more and more often, so he and his father could laugh about it together. Then the lesson began to spread into real life, like a bad cold that everybody with testosterone caught.

"Clean up the den," I'd command. "This house looks like a pigsty."

"Look the other way!" one or both of the males in our house would reply.

Wipe your feet. Comb your hair. Brush your teeth.

"Look the other way!"

Long after our son learned to read for himself, Henry the Duck still stalks our house, assuming a duck can stalk. After all these years, I'm a little irritated with Henry and his two sidekicks, and I'm threatening to write a sequel with a new moral so we can all read it together.

Think of it. Rainbow Brite and the Berenstain Bears are speeding along when they see a pedestrian crossing the street. They honk their horn, but it's too late. Poor Henry the Duck looked the other way.

Creating Havoc

When my husband and I want our children to feel sorry for us, we tell them about our childhoods. They're in a state of shock by the time we finish.

We didn't have personal computers, we say, or digital television or cell phones or the grunge look or in-line skates. We had to add and subtract and multiply and divide *in our heads* because we didn't have tiny calculators, and we actually had to tie our own shoes because no one had even heard of Velcro.

By this time, as I said, our children are practically in shock. Or maybe they're giggling hysterically. The point is, they're already feeling extremely emotional when I tell them the most alarming fact about our childhood.

"When your father and I were children," I say, *"no one cared if we were creative or not.* Our parents and teachers wanted us to be neat and clean and well behaved, and we were supposed to work hard and learn a lot. But no one ever told us about creativity."

This is our kids' cue to leave the room or go into a deep stupor. They already know that I get a little too excited about the whole creativity issue. After a few minutes, I'll have to be propped in a corner and fed bread crumbs for a week.

Creativity! My daughter brings home a writing assignment. "Be creative," it says. My son works on an art project. He's supposed to be creative, too. The schools, the extracurricular groups, and the enrichment classes all want creativity, as well.

"Do something creative with this piece of rope," I once heard another mother tell a group of ten-year-olds. She pushed a foot-long span of rope across the table, and the children stared back blankly at her. Finally one of the boys tied a knot in the rope, and the woman consulted a book and shook her head. "That's a *common* use," she said. "It's not a *creative* use."

The mother looked at me and shook her head again. She wanted my advice because she'd already decided I was the "creative" type. That's what people call you when you do the kind of work you don't get paid much money for. I didn't say anything, because I was already kind of apoplectic after hearing words like "common" and "creative" bandied about and quantified as easily as a heat wave on a thermometer.

Be creative! I get the vapors just thinking about it. I can't think of a worse thing to tell children if you want them to do something artistic or interesting or offbeat. Tell them to have fun with a project. Tell them to play with it or do something strange or different if they feel like it. Tell them to look at the world upside-down, inside-out. Tell them anything, but don't tell them to be creative.

The truth is, I can't think of anything that kills creativity as quickly as being commanded to come up with it and then being graded on it. It's like being told to be happy—or else.

What a shame, too. There's so much joy and exhilaration in wholeheartedly plunging into a project and becoming so immersed that hours pass without your noticing. I can't think of a more satisfying pleasure for children than to lose themselves in a drawing or a book or an imaginary world.

But we don't have that. Instead, we've got the Creativity Police with their foot-long ropes and textbook standards, and I'm convinced they're making our children self-conscious and timid and uncertain, and they're giving me a facial tic.

The trouble is, you can't always take the most direct route to where you want to go. Sometimes, you have to go backward or the long way around to get there. That's what I'm trying to teach my kids, anyway.

You might do something creative if you forget all about being creative.

You might be happy if you stop trying so hard to be happy.

And you might learn more math if you throw away your calculator.

The Deep End

I didn't take swimming lessons because of my fortieth birthday. I'd like to blame it on that, but it isn't true. I took them because of my seven-year-old daughter, Teal. I could see it in her eyes. She already hated the water as much as I did.

"We're going to take swimming lessons together," I told her. I tried to sound loud and enthusiastic. "It'll be fun. We'll have a great time."

Teal looked unimpressed. Maybe I hadn't talked loudly enough. "I don't know, Mommy," she said. "I hate putting my head underwater."

Good point, I thought. I'd always found putting my head underwater to be particularly revolting.

"But you'll learn to like it," I said. "Just wait. You'll come to love the water."

Two weeks later Teal didn't look any happier when we had our first lesson. The chlorine hurt her eyes. The glare on the water was too bright. She couldn't relax enough to float. When the instructor asked her to jump off the side of the pool into the water, she refused and cried, instead.

A few yards away, I splashed in the shallow end. I did my version of the breaststroke for the instructor. I floated. I decided I didn't loathe the water when it was quite shallow.

"I had fun, didn't you?" I said to Teal as we dried off.

"Why do we have to take swimming lessons?" she said. "I hate them."

"We're taking them because the water's fun and everyone should learn to swim," I announced. "And because it's such a drag not knowing how to swim. I don't want you to go through that."

I should know. I'd spent a lifetime not knowing how to swim. I'd grown from childhood to adulthood without leaving the shallow end.

I wasn't sure why. I'd always wished I could pin my fears of the water onto something traumatic. But I couldn't. I'd never even had a bad experience in the bathtub. And it's hard to come close to drowning, even in a pool, when you're standing in only two feet of water and your hands are firmly attached to dry land—just in case.

Ten years ago I'd taken swimming lessons for the last time. It was hopeless. I could see that from the beginning. I first became suspicious of the instructor when he told me I needed to relax in the water or I'd never float. Worse, he urged me to float on my back, which I considered to be quite unnatural. I tried to explain that I didn't even like to lie on my back on waterbeds.

Weeks passed, and we were at an impasse. The instructor tried to talk me into going to the deep end. I told him I didn't want to, because people drowned in deep water all the time.

He said yes, but that was how people learned to swim. And didn't I want to learn?

I told him that, no, come to think of it, I really didn't. Later I'd written an article about the trauma of taking swimming lessons. Two people wrote me letters. One said he loved my writing and I should write a novel. The second said I was so messed up that I should join his water therapy group immediately.

Anyway, I'd always tried to joke about not knowing how to swim. But when it came down to it, it wasn't funny at all—and I didn't want my daughter to have to live that way. I wanted her to learn to swim this summer, while she was still young. Most of all, I didn't want to infect her with my own fears and doubts.

But watching her, I saw a younger version of myself grimacing when she got into the water and choking when she put her head under. I loudly encouraged every small bit of progress she made. Head under water for five seconds? Great. Didn't hate it as much this time? Fantastic. Almost floated? Wonderful.

"You'll be swimming like crazy by the end of the summer," I kept telling her. "And so will I."

Fat chance, I thought. She's as unteachable as I am.

Three weeks later Teal jumped off the diving board for the first time and swam freestyle to the other end of the pool. She loved it, she said, and jumped off four more times.

Afterward I bought her a small ice cream with M&Ms mixed in. I bought myself a large one, with Oreos mixed in.

"Jumping off the diving board is so much fun, Mommy," she said.

I watched her over the next few days as she grew more and more confident in the water. She had mastered the freestyle and moved on to the butterfly, the breaststroke, and the backstroke.

She moved quickly in the water, her head bobbing up for air occasionally. Her brightly colored swimsuit flashed in the sunlight, and somehow she held herself differently, even out of the water. I still encouraged her loudly from the side of the pool, but I could tell she didn't need it as much.

"You may not be interested," the instructor said, "but I think she could swim competitively if she wanted to. She's that good."

"That good?" I echoed wonderingly.

On my own, I tried to stay in the shallow end. But sometimes I ventured into the deep water. I sat on the edge of the pool and sometimes I jumped in and managed to make it to the other side. I still wondered why people insisted on making swimming pools so deep. It struck me as a dangerous and perverse practice. I was much happier swimming in the shallow water.

I was sitting on the step in the deep end one day. Teal dared me to go off the diving board. I got up and stood at the edge of the pool, then on the diving board. I looked down into the deep blue water. The usual danger signals went off.

"Mommy!" Teal called. "You can do it, Mommy! You can jump off."

I looked at her, faintly sunburned and confident and happy. She was bobbing up and down in the deep end. "You can do it!" she said again.

I peered down into the water again. It isn't supposed to be this way, I thought. This wasn't turning out as I'd planned it. It would take all her allowance to buy me ice cream if I jumped off the board.

Did I really want an ice cream—even a large one—that much?

I put my hands together and bent over. The water, I noticed, was still as deep as ever.

———— 🍎 ————

Pacing the Sidelines

The parents are psyched. We walk up and down the field. We grit our teeth and scream and applaud. We contort our bodies and make little kicking motions. By the time the soccer game's over, we're exhausted.

Usually I pace the side of the field with my friends Geoff and Paul. Our spouses sit more sedately in the stands and pretend they don't know who we are. At least Geoff's and my spouses do. Paul is divorced, and he's actively looking for a spouse who will ignore him.

Most games, Geoff and Paul and I stay at the end of the field where our sons' team needs to score. We think this helps. If we stay at that end of the field and make enough racket, we'll exert some kind of irresistible force field, we like to think.

So far this season our theory's working. Our sons' team, Lightning, has won all its games but one. "They're really playing like a team"—that's what all the parents chortle to each other when we stand around, gloating, at the end of the games. "Maybe all those years of losing have built character and solidarity."

Maybe. Or maybe it's having a female coach this season. One theory that's making the parental rounds is that it's been helpful for our newly teenage boys to have a woman as a coach. I think this theory has something to do with hormones. Which makes sense to me, because if it's anything boys this age have, it's hormones.

"The boys relate well to a female coach, because they all have such aggressive mothers. They're used to following orders their mothers give them"—that's another theory that's wafting around. I think one of the parents who's a psychologist came up with it, which is a safe bet, since half the team's parents are psychologists.

But aggressive mothers? I have no inkling where that idea came from. I look up and down the field and don't see any aggressive mothers. Most of the mothers are bellowing from the bleachers and behind the fence and jumping up and down and giving each other high-fives. That's not aggressive, Dr. Freud. That's *motherhood*.

The game goes on, and Paul almost gets in a fight with some of the parents from the other team. "Get down here and score some more goals, Lightning!" he's been screaming.

Since our team is already ahead by two or three points, the other side takes umbrage. "How many goals do you need?"

somebody shouts back. I try to act like I don't know Paul. Who's this guy with, anyway?

Last week Geoff was the one who got a little overly excited on the sidelines. The team was down at the half, and they were playing like they were sleepwalking. "We didn't drive all the way to Round Rock to watch you play like this!" Geoff yelled when they were all lined up for the second half.

My husband and Geoff's wife thought Geoff had gone a bit too far with that remark. But I think they're wrong. *Was it any coincidence that our team rallied and won the game in the second half?* I don't think so. "Geoff did what he had to do," I tell them.

As for me, I try not to yell too much. I'm under strict orders from my son not to humiliate him.

Besides, if you want to know the truth, I'm kind of a former soccer player myself. A few years ago I played briefly on a women's indoor team, and I know what the pressure's like. I'll never forget the first time we lined up on the field for our very first game, facing the other team eyeball-to-eyeball. This is emblazoned in my memory as the only time in my life I wished I weighed more.

My son used to come to my games. He was in the bleachers the night another player bashed into me and I went flying. I worried about that for a while. What deep psychological wound would it inflict on him in his adulthood—seeing his mother careening through the air, like a bowling ball out of control? Then I stopped worrying about it. I realized it was probably much more traumatic to have a mother who was such a crummy player.

Today my son scores twice. The parents jump up and down and screech and hug each other. Even my husband's on his feet, I notice.

"Did you see? He scored left-footed," I tell Paul.

Paul nods. He looks tired. The team looks tired, too, flush-faced and slower moving. So do all the rest of the parents.

It's exhausting, you know. When you're our age and you have to exert all that effort and magnetism and noise and irresistible force from the side of the field, you feel it the next morning.

But right now, we've all got a spring in our step. *Another victory.* The way I look at it, we've all done our part.

The Dinner Hour

Dinner! That's the secret! You know that because you've heard it everywhere. On Oprah, probably. *Families who regularly eat dinner together are closer and happier and their kids don't sport as many tattoos, body piercings, or felonies.* Something like that.

Which is why you and your husband try so hard to get the four of you together for dinner as often as possible. But when you have two teenage children, it isn't easy to find a dinnertime. You have to thread your way through a maze of soccer practices, music lessons, lacrosse, debate tournaments, school newspaper deadlines, research meetings, and support groups. That's why you don't get together for dinner every night. You'd be eating at midnight.

But anyway, tonight you're eating at home, and it isn't even close to midnight. Your husband is chopping up a bunch of chile peppers to grill with the fish, and you are making a salad, since no one trusts you to cook. Everything is almost ready.

You scream for your son to set the table. Silence. You scream again. He emerges and sets the table grudgingly. He is, he announces loudly, the only child in this family who does any work at all. He should be getting a much bigger allowance than his older sister, who does nothing but lie around, talk on the phone, watch television, and do her homework. But no. He is treated like dirt, just because he is younger.

For some reason, that makes you think of an old friend of yours who moved back to Boston a few years ago. She used to say her parents had three children because they couldn't afford servants. You always wondered about that statement. *What did those people know that you don't? What was their secret?*

Dinner is ready. You and your husband both scream for the kids to come. After much browbeating, the four of you sit down.

"What are we having?" your daughter asks. She looks different now that she's finally disconnected her ear from the phone. "Oh, *yecccchh*. You know I hate salmon."

The phone rings. Your son leaps up to answer it.

"I'm not here," your daughter hisses at him. "Take a message."

He nods. He's notorious for losing everyone else's telephone messages, but he always dutifully records them for his sister. That is because she has promised to track him down and kill him if he doesn't.

Your son takes a message and sits down again. The four of you start to eat.

"I had the most interesting research findings today," your husband begins.

"*Bor-rrrrring*," your daughter announces.

The phone rings again. Your son jumps up. The phone stops ringing before he gets to it. He stomps back to his chair in a huff.

Your daughter, who's seventeen, shakes her head. "When is he going to get over this adolescence thing?" she asks.

Your son quickly recovers and tells a story about how his class went through some kind of security drill at school. The punch line revolves around another student's flatulence. This is true of every single one of his punch lines these days, you have noticed. By the time he's finished his story, he's laughing so hard he can barely sit up.

"Is that supposed to be funny?" your daughter asks, rolling her eyes. She starts talking about what she is learning at school. They're reading a book by Michel Foucault.

You realize you have absolutely nothing intelligent to say about Michel Foucault, although you have a dim memory that he wrote about sex. You also realize that you never, ever read books by racy people like Michel Foucault when you were in high school. Oh, no. You read books like *Silas Marner* and *The Return of the Native* about 500 times so you could understand the symbolism of a pitchfork or something and become a life-long Anglophobe who has frequent nightmares about farming implements.

Your daughter is still talking. You've noticed a pattern here. The longer she's been in debate, the more she's been talking. (Debate! Why did you encourage it? Oh, that's right. You were worried about all that research about adolescent girls' plunge in self-esteem. Note to self: *This is no longer a concern*.)

Dinner is over. You know that because all of a sudden everyone else has left the table. They have homework! Meetings! Obligations! No time to help clean up.

You think about that while you load the dishwasher. Maybe you should get in touch with your friend from Boston again. She knows something you need to learn.

Time Management Can't Start Too Young

"What can parents do to help their children figure out how to make the best choices, set priorities, get done what needs to be done, and still have time to be a kid? ... Even toddlers can start learning about how to manage their time."
— *"Time Management for Kids,"*
Better Homes & Gardens, *October 2000*

HELLO, PARENTS!

Is this a familiar scene at your house?

- Eighteen-month-old Caitlin is late to all her appointments because she lacks the necessary self-discipline to plan ahead. It's one-fifteen, and she's still not ready for her one o'clock play date with Robbie. Right now, she's looking for her "blankie" and she's using her outdoors voice inside the house and she has to go to the bathroom (again!). When you call Robbie's mother to apologize for being so disorganized and late, you can tell she's irritated at both of you.

No wonder! Robbie's always on time. Robbie's always well organized. Robbie doesn't have a childish, neurotic dependence on a blankie.

At the rate he's going, Robbie will probably get into Harvard. And Caitlin? Well, do the words "paper or plastic?" mean anything to you?

BUT WAIT. IT'S NOT TOO LATE!!!

Sure, Caitlin seems to be a hopeless case at her age. But, believe me, we at SUPERCHILD TIME-MANAGEMENT have seen worse. (Toddlers who don't wear wristwatches and can't tell time! Who don't even know what a color-coded

19

calendar or a Palm Pilot is! As you can imagine, their parents were frantic. *Where had they gone wrong?*)

Let us be frank, though. Behind every tardy, daydreaming, wayward toddler, there's a family that needs our help.

There's a mother whose hem is dragging and lipstick is smeared. That's probably why she never finished her MBA and doesn't even have her own child's baby book up to date. Worse, she never takes the time to ask herself the question every good mother needs to ask as frequently as possible: *What am I doing wrong that will warp my child forever and cause her to be a failure in life?*

And Daddy? Oh, yeah. Isn't he that wild-eyed loser who just bolted out the front door with a fresh coffee spill on his tie and a bled-through band-aid where he almost dismembered himself shaving? As usual, he's late to his first appointment, his car's out of gas, and he's got a wad of used dental floss stuck to his shoe. Sad, isn't it?

This is why we at SUPERCHILD TIME-MANAGEMENT believe disorganization is a deep-seated family flaw. We want to work with you and your family to help you mend your haphazard ways before disaster strikes and you have a kindergartner who doesn't know the meaning of the word "prioritize."

Among the time-management principles we will teach you:

- ◆ The language of organization. How to give your toddler the right choices!

BAD EXAMPLE:

"What do you want to do right now, Caitlin? Mommy's going to take a nap."

(Little Caitlin is looking up to Mommy to provide her with structure and organizational skills—and what's Mommy doing? She's sleeping on the job and may, indeed, have a secret drinking problem or issues about her position as an authority figure that need to be worked out. When you ask a child what she wants to do, she very rarely answers, "Clean my room" or "Let's sit down and plan the rest of the week together, Mommy!" This is one very good reason why you should never ask children what they want to do. They always want to do the wrong things.)

GOOD EXAMPLE:

"Caitlin, would you rather help Mommy organize your closet or help Mommy color-coordinate your stuffed animals?"

(Here, Mommy is giving Caitlin freedom of choice within reason—something every rational, mature, Ivy League-bound 18-month-old can understand and appreciate. Mommy is also showing Caitlin that she has her priorities straight and doesn't waste her time reading books, daydreaming, or talking with her friends on the phone. No, Mommy is organized and efficient!)

* How to reward your child with nifty treats such as gum with a little caffeine in it (especially effective for that sluggish child who holds back the rest of the family!) and special toddler-model briefcases, to-do lists, and Palm Pilots for Small Palms.

REMEMBER, no family is hopeless! Let us put you and your toddler on the fast track to organization, time management, more play dates at Robbie's, and a new, productive, efficient family—*yours*!—that never files extensions on its tax returns.

P.S. By the way, it's a complete myth that organized people aren't a lot of fun to be around. We at SUPERCHILD are a zany bunch who have barrels of fun during our regularly scheduled "Get Loosey-Goosey and Wild!" appointments every day from 4:15 to 4:30 P.M. You'd be surprised how much fun you can have in fifteen minutes—as long as you plan ahead!

John, Paul, George, and Ringo

Oh, sure. It was cute at first.

When our children started to get interested in the Beatles, I actually thought it was sweet. I think that was because we'd just spent last summer's vacation driving around the mountains and every five minutes our kids would demand to hear some horrible song over and over. They seemed to be listening to singers who—as far as I could tell—expressed their total alienation from the universe by moping and whining a lot.

Most of the time they wanted to hear a song called "Isn't it Ironic?" I occasionally announced that I didn't think the song was that ironic if you want to get technical, but no one paid any attention to me. So I privately changed the name of the song to "Isn't It Bubonic?" and made up my own lyrics. (*It's like fleas that bite... when your dog is awaaay! A little plague... that you just can't shaaaake!*)

Anyway, that's why I was so naïve and unprepared when my kids started to appreciate the Beatles. They'd ask me simple questions about the Beatles, such as what their names were or who was singing the lead on this song or that, and I would patiently explain. They would ask me who the most talented Beatle was and I would get to tell them my own personal theory that—contrary to mistaken popular belief—it was Paul. Definitely Paul.

I love to expand on my own personal theories, especially when someone actually listens to me for a change. Paul was always underrated, I would tell them darkly. No one gave him enough musical or intellectual credit, just because he was so good-looking. Just because he had those gorgeous, soulful eyes and that traffic-stopping, innocent face. Even though I was a teeming, overheated mass of adolescent hormones at the time, I hinted, I didn't focus on Paul's good looks. No, I appreciated him for his musical genius, that's all. Someday the rest of the world would catch up.

The summer passed, and we listened to Beatles CDs and tapes. We watched every volume of the videotaped *Beatles Anthology*. When we drove anywhere, the kids would demand to listen to the Beatles. Like I said, it was cute at first. But so was Macaulay Culkin, and look what happened to him.

After a while the kids stopped asking my husband and me what the best Beatles album was (*Rubber Soul* or *Sergeant Pepper*) and what their greatest song was ("You Won't See Me" or "Yesterday" or "In My Life"). Instead, they began to come up with their own opinions. "'Let It Be' is their greatest song," our daughter said. They even started questioning my judgment about Paul's being the most talented Beatle. "I like John the best," our son announced. "He was the smartest one."

That's when I knew it had gone too far. It wasn't cute any longer. As a matter of fact, it wasn't even amusing.

I talked to my brother-in-law in Houston, and he reported that his kids liked the Beatles, too. Everywhere I turned, I heard about more and more teenagers who loved the Beatles.

Wait a minute, I kept thinking. The Beatles belong to our generation, not theirs. We're the ones who discovered them. Understand?

Besides, at least *we* took some initiative when *we* were teenagers. You didn't see us glomming onto Glenn Miller and dancing to "Moonlight Serenade," did you? No way. We had too much pride. We went out and carefully selected bands and music we knew our parents would hate.

What's wrong with kids these days? They're supposed to be rebelling against us and now they're letting us down. Don't they know they're messing with the natural order of parent-child relations? We, the parents, are supposed to loathe their music. But how can we when it's John, Paul, George, and

Ringo? How can we complain about it when it's such great music?

Or could this all be a trick? That's what I wonder in my darker, more cynical moments. Maybe they're trying to drive their parents' generation nuts by loving the music we love. Wouldn't that be sneaky and underhanded? Wouldn't that be subversive?

Okay, I get it now. A failure to rebel must be the ultimate rebellion when your parents come from a rebellious generation. Rebelling by conforming. Now that I think of it, how ironic can you get?

—————— 🍎 ——————

Don't Go Retro on Me

I always heard that the toughest thing about having children is that you want to save them from making the same dumb mistakes you made. But I never believed it until this year, when 1970s clothes came back into style.

The '70s! Why are fashion designers doing this to us? Sure, it was a great decade for movies and political scandals, but it was hideous time for clothes.

David Letterman calls it the ugliest decade in the history of the world, and he sometimes shows pictures to prove his point. Those pictures are what I consider compelling scientific evidence: We all looked horrible in the '70s, even if we didn't realize it at the time. Everybody's hair was cut like a French poodle's fur, and our clothes fit so tightly that we all looked like pastel pipe cleaners.

(If you don't believe me, look at a picture of yourself from that decade and ask, *How could anyone that young look that bad?*

Then, after the nausea passes, destroy the picture as quickly as possible.)

So cut it out, kids! Stop punishing your parents! If you're going to be retro, don't go back to the '70s. Try a better-looking decade or the Dark Ages or something.

But nobody is listening to me. I go shopping with my teen-age daughter, and I spend most of my time cringing, hanging on to the clothes racks, and developing a serious facial tic.

Aaaaggghh, I think. *Stay away from that chartreuse polyester blouse! It's revolting. Bell-bottom pants are vile, too! They make anyone's ankles look obese, especially when you wear them with those wretched platform shoes that weigh about 400 pounds apiece and probably give you dangerous foot problems like ingrown toenails.*

I don't say anything, of course. That's because I am trying not to be a controlling mother. I take a lot of deep breaths and practice sending silent warning messages—emergency fash-ion bulletins—which my daughter doesn't seem to hear.

It must be my fault, I finally realize. If I were a good fashion role model, my daughter wouldn't want to wear '70s clothes. She'd understand what a big mistake it is. But I am a terrible fashion role model. I never learned to accessorize, and I can't tie a scarf right, and my hem usually drags, and my stockings run, which is why I spend most of my life in exercise clothes. That way, people will at least think I'm fit.

In fact, I've developed only two tips for stylish dressing over the course of my entire life. First, I often wear black in the remote hope that someone might think I'm sophisticated.

Second—and this is what I consider to be my personal acid test—I always ask myself: *If I wear this, will I have to hold in my stomach?* I never buy anything that requires me to hold in my stomach, since I think that leads to lots of severe personal-ity problems. Most of the '70s clothes forced you to hold in your stomach, which explains why everyone in that decade was also in therapy.

But, anyway. My daughter comes home with platform shoes that are as big as cross-country skis and a lot noisier. She says she loves these new styles. Maybe it's too late for her, I think sadly.

I watch our ten-year-old son. So far, he doesn't seem affected. He still wears the same T-shirts and sweat pants he always did. But I'm watching him very carefully so I can see early signs of the '70s creeping in. I'm going to be vigilant. If I turn my back for just five minutes, he might grow sideburns and start wearing a green pastel leisure suit with a ruffled shirt. The next thing I know, he'll look just like Tony Orlando and will go around singing songs like "Tie a Yellow Ribbon 'Round the Old Oak Tree."

If he shows any signs of this kind of behavior, I'm going to play hardball. I'll get out a picture of his father and me from the '70s. Maybe, just maybe, our children can learn from our mistakes when the evidence looks this bad.

Chapter 2

Pregnancy and Motherhood, Multiplication and Division

Equal Opportunities:

A Pause for a Brief Nine-and-a-Half Month Interlude from the Perspectives of a Pregnant Woman and Her Husband

Month One

HERS: Get up. Lurch into bathroom. Wonder briefly why stomach's upset. Decide it was last night's enchiladas at Chez Fernandez.

Stumble into kitchen. Coffee, that's what you need. Pour a cup. Quickly realize it makes you sick. Rush back to bathroom.

Return to bed. Resolve never to go to Chez Fernandez again.

HIS: Back from jogging. Three miles in 35 minutes. Not bad for someone your age. Not bad at all.

Notice wife is still in bed. Tell her how well you've run. No reply. Nag her about how she should go jogging with you; then she wouldn't be so tired all the time.

Wife pulls covers over her head. Tell her she's being passive-aggressive. Should communicate feelings better.

Covers don't move.

Month Two

HERS: Couldn't be—could I? Just that one time when we got carried away. Certain it was safe. After all, rhythm method works for millions of Catholics. Millions and millions and millions of Catholics.

Consider idea of baby. Tiny little fingers. Precious little sweaters. Start to sniffle, just thinking about it. A baby!

Wonder how husband will react. Always saying, we'll start family once we buy house. (Where will baby sleep in a one-bedroom apartment? What does Dr. Spock say about babies raised in walk-in closet?) Start to sob just thinking about it.

Decide to make appointment with OB, just in case.

HIS: What does wife mean, she might be pregnant?

Look around OB's waiting room. Notice all the other women appear to be extremely pregnant. Hope none of them goes into labor while you're here.

Think about it—a baby! A son in the prime of your life! Can tell wife's skittish about it, though. Kept saying she wanted to wait a few years—get her career off to a good start.

Nurse comes out. Calls your name. Look around. Maybe there's another Mr. Bridgebottom in waiting room.

Apparently not.

Go into doctor's room. Wife looks happy. Doctor looks pompous. No wonder they get sued all the time.

Congratulations, doctor says.

Month Three

HERS: Sick three times this afternoon. Wonder who in hell named it morning sickness.

Breasts bigger, stomach starting to show. Next-door neighbor says get ready for varicose veins and stretch marks, honey. You'll look like road map of Manhattan. Throw out bikinis, too.

Get out copy of the *Astonishing Life of the Fetus*. Size of your thumb now, it says. Brain forming. Eyes, ears developing. Moving around, but so small you can't feel it.

Start to cry, just looking at thumb. Fall asleep.

HIS: Wife's crabby again. Gives you lots of long-suffering looks and big sighs. O'Feeney warned you about this—wife goes bonkers for nine months solid.

Note wife's fallen asleep again. Pick up copy of *The Astonishing Life of the Fetus*. Examine thumb.

Month Four

HERS: Tired of zippers splitting. Time to buy maternity clothes. Resolve to buy beautiful, chic outfits. Begin to prepare for compliments: "You look stunning!" "I didn't know maternity clothes could be so stylish!"

Grab fistful of credit cards. Head to La Jolie Mere "Because you Expect the Beautiful" Boutique.

Wade through racks of gingham smocks with ruffles and bows. T-shirts with arrows pointing down from word "Baby." Ask saleswoman where maternity dress-for-success look is. She points to three-piece gingham suit with white blouse and bow.

HIS: Notice wife is dressing strangely these days. Funny, she never used to like bows and ruffles. Maybe women's tastes change when they get pregnant. Decide not to ask, though. Has another one of those dark looks on her face.

Return to more pressing matters: what to name baby. Look at *Book of Better Baby Names*. Alistair? Too effete. Elvis? Too dead. Henry? Nope. Reminds you of Henry "Pinhead" Perzersky at Central High.

Shake head with despair. Two thousand names—and you wouldn't call your hamster one of them. Want something strong and distinctive—just like your name.

Wait! That's it! Junior! John Junior!

Month Five

HERS: Prepare for monthly doctor's visit and weigh-in. Skip breakfast, wear light cotton dress, take shoes off before getting on scales. Six more pounds. Scales must be wrong, you say. No, says nurse, scales are accurate and you'd better watch it. Inform nurse that twins run in the family—certain that's why you're gaining so much weight. Nurse looks doubtful. Tell her stubbornly you're going to name them Catherine and Nicholas.

Doctor more cheerful. Says forget about twins, though. Only one heartbeat. Forget about jelly doughnuts, too, he says. Unless you want to look like one.

HIS: Watch wife eat dinner. Wonder whether she was a vacuum cleaner in past life. Two cheeseburgers. French fries. Strawberry malt. Ask self whether this would be a good time to tactfully remind her about her weight again. Decide not to.

Finally, she finishes second cheeseburger and wipes face with napkin. What's for dessert? she says.

Month Six

HERS: Day started wrong when couldn't get your seat belt around stomach. At coffee break, Marie in accounting talks about cousin's five-day labor. A living hell. And you know something? Marie says. You're built just like her.

Resolve never to talk to anyone who's had a baby or knows anyone who's had a baby. Get in car and head home. Car breaks down on freeway. Sit there and cry.

HIS: Remind self to tell wife car needs gas.

Month Seven

HERS: 3:12 A.M. Take fifth trip to bathroom—new record. Return to bed. Sleeping on stomach anatomically impossible. Sleeping on back makes heartburn worse. Decide to go with heartburn and turn on back. Catherine/Nicholas starts to kick. Dream you've having litter of puppies.

HIS: ZZZZZZZZZZ

Month Eight

HERS: Go to first meeting of YMCA Prepared Childbirth Course. Sit on floor with six other pregnant women and spouses.

Instructor, Becky, is suspiciously enthusiastic. Explains how French doctor Fernand Lamaze discovered no need for drugs—just proper breathing—during labor. Now women can fully experience childbirth. Resist urge to ask how many childbirths Dr. Lamaze fully experienced.

HIS: Try to listen to Lamaze instructor. Betty or somebody. Clearly one of those all-natural fruitcakes. Recall what it was like when you were born. All men had to do was hang around in the waiting room and pace and go to a bar to get drunk and hand out cigars.

But not you! Oh, no. Just your luck! Wife gets pregnant in age of equality—time of great oppression of men. Now women want to drag men into delivery room. Not sure why. Wife starts screaming about how much pain she'll be in and least you could do is show up to watch. Besides, men should feel grateful they can witness miracle of birth and be childbirth coaches.

Perk up at mention of coaches. Realize this will be first of many times coaching John Jr. John Jr. slides into third. John Jr. makes winning touchdown pass. John Jr. gets born.

Plan to buy "COACH" sweatshirt immediately.

Month Nine

HERS: Could be any day now. Should take some kind of decisive action. Pack hospital bag, maybe.

Decide to lie down instead. Wonder if baby will like walk-in closet. Try to imagine what Catherine/Nicholas will look like. Realize you don't deserve to have baby because you'll be such an awful mother. Start to cry (fourth time today). Roll over and go to sleep.

HIS: Check watch—9 P.M. Wife's already asleep. Damn. Wanted to turn up television really loud so John Jr. could hear game. Want him to get used to roar of the crowd.

Month Nine-and-a-Half

HERS: Consult pregnancy book. Note that one pregnancy in ten lasts as long as yours. Wonderful.

Phone rings. Marie. Still at home? Doesn't baby know it's due? she asks.

Slam down phone. Scream that you want unlisted number. Tired of talking to busybodies all the time. Husband screams back he can't talk till game's over.

Look around house. A mess, as usual. Sling water, soap everywhere. Wash dishes, scrub pots, pans, refrigerator. Stop to consider whether this is nesting syndrome.

Floor's wet. Funny. Thought you'd just mopped it dry.

HIS: Top of the ninth. Best game you've seen all season. No-hitter so far.

Racket from the kitchen. Strange. Wife hasn't been in there for months. Making so much noise, you can hardly hear game.

Will pitcher pull this one off? Think maybe you should have followed heart and gone into majors instead of accounting. Should never have listened to that coach. That scumbag. Hope John Jr. gets coach who recognizes his talent.

Wife's yelling again. Something about labor. Yell back she shouldn't work so hard, then. Should hire a maid.

Game so exciting, you can't believe it. Jeter blasts one to right field, fielder slips and misses it. Runner's stealing third, then heading home. Right fielder recovers, throws a hard one to—

Labor?

Some of the Only Stories that Matter

When I was pregnant with my first child, my friend Katey gave me lots of advice. Katey already had two children, so she was an expert. She was also very bossy, and she loved giving advice, even when I didn't ask for it. Every time she told me something, I wondered if motherhood made you bossy.

One of Katey's favorite topics was her theory about why women who had had babies loved to tell their stories about pregnancy and childbirth.

"We talk about childbirth and pregnancy the same way men talk about war," she said. "Childbirth is a woman's war story."

Katey probably told me that theory several million times while I was pregnant, and I always thought how unenlightened it was. Sexist, even. Women had been prevented from going to war; it was a right we still had to fight for. It wasn't our fault we didn't have any war stories. Our own tales of childbirth and pregnancy, in comparison, were poor substitutes.

But I usually didn't argue with Katey. I had too many other things to worry about, such as the fact that if I didn't give birth soon, I'd probably be in the *Guinness Book of World Records* for the longest pregnancy in the history of the Earth. Every time Katey brought up her theory again, I'd practice my Lamaze breathing and start to hyperventilate.

Since then I managed to give birth twice, I never made it into *Guinness*, and Katey and I both moved. But I still think about her theory, even though she's not around to remind me of it. It's like a splinter I can't get rid of.

I thought about it last week, in fact, when I was at a shower for Renee, a friend whose first baby is due in November. Every time I opened my mouth, I noticed, I was reminiscing about my own pregnancies and childbirth and giving advice no one had asked for. Come to think of it, I sounded a lot like Katey.

The sonograms of Renee's baby boy—they're so much clearer than they were when I was pregnant!

The maternity clothes. They're so much better! They don't have those nasty little bows at the neck any longer!

I talked and I talked. I talked about the first time you hear the baby's heartbeat. The stretch marks. The doctor's visits. The medical tests, the waiting, the preparation classes. The emotional upheavals. I found myself telling anyone who would listen how I'd cry—no, *sob*!—every time I saw a really moving commercial on TV when I was pregnant.

"Childbirth is the most extraordinary experience you'll ever have," I told Renee's husband, Robert, before I left. He hadn't asked me about it, but I thought he should know.

Walking home, I thought about women and pregnancy and childbirth, and this compulsion so many of us have to talk about it. I still didn't agree with Katey, exactly. These weren't our war stories—but they weren't poor substitutes, either, as I'd once thought.

So what were they to us, anyway? Maybe they were stories of a time when we were suddenly aware of being a part of something larger—of this vast procession of birth and life. They were stories we needed to tell, again and again, so we could understand them ourselves.

I could see myself and Katey and Renee and lots of other friends, growing older and grayer and still telling those stories to anyone who'd listen. Still telling them, because we finally realized we'd lived through one of the few stories on Earth that really mattered.

———— 🍎 ————

The Stork Parks Here

Reserved parking for pregnant women? During my first pregnancy in 1981, I would have been insulted by it.

That was a time when professional women were trying to prove they were just the same as men, so most of us went around wearing those awful little junior-men outfits with pinstripes and perky little ties and pretending that earned run averages were a fascinating topic of conversation. When we turned up pregnant, we overcompensated. We worked harder. We never complained. We didn't want any special favors.

Reserved parking for pregnant women? Four years later, during my second pregnancy, I would have committed a felony to get it.

By then I was tired of the whole Pregnant Superwoman routine I had put on before. I was just tired, period. Forget overcompensation. Forget stoicism, too. I worked hard, but I also complained a lot. (That was one of the prerogatives of pregnancy, I decided. You could complain a lot and develop a very bad personality, and everyone would think it was temporary—just like those stretch marks that were supposed to go away if you used Vaseline.)

"Take advantage of your pregnancy," I told a friend. She was expecting her first baby, and it was clear she needed my advice. "Nobody's going to pamper you when you get home from the hospital with your baby."

"You already told me that five times," she said.

Anyway, that was my frame of mind eleven years ago, when I lost an argument with a security guard at Dallas Love Field about all of this. It happened late one night as I was sitting in my car, waiting to pick up my husband. Our four-year-old daughter was asleep in the back seat, and I was crouched behind the steering wheel, exhausted and extremely pregnant. We were parked in one of the only vacant spaces, all of which were marked handicapped.

"You've got to keep moving, lady," the security guard said, tapping on my window. "This is a handicapped space."

"I'm seven months pregnant," I pointed out. "Doesn't that seem kind of handicapped to you?"

It was the wrong thing to say. A gigantic mistake. The security guard glared at me like I was Eva Braun hiding out in a maternity dress and jumbo pantyhose. So much for chivalry.

"Pregnant isn't handicapped," he said. "Keep moving, lady."

I drove off in a huff, muttering and wondering aloud how this guy, *this insensitive, sexist lout*, would like to spend a few months with morning sickness, varicose veins, stretch marks, a squashed bladder, and a bowling ball strapped to his midriff. Then we'd see how non-handicapped he felt.

Naturally, I remembered this security guard when I read about a few Dallas-area stores that now reserve parking spaces for pregnant women. Hallelujah! I thought. It's about time! We've finally come to the realization that the workplace won't screech to a halt with pregnant women in it and that women's rights won't take a permanent nose dive if a pregnant woman admits she needs more sleep or somewhere to prop her feet or a better parking space. Maybe it's a little inconvenient, but I think the rest of us can handle it.

In fact, I'd like to think this is only the beginning. I envision reserved maternity parking at every grocery store and movie theater, every doctor's office and restaurant, every school and workplace. I see better-looking maternity clothes! More public bathrooms! Laws against stretch marks! No more episiotomy stitches! Shorter labors!

I can even see special parking for expectant mothers at an airport here in town. When your name is Love, it seems to me you have an obligation to clear a few places for the consequences of love.

———————— 🍎 ————————

As Natural as Childbirth

Everybody's getting epidurals during childbirth these days. From 1981 to 1997, I read recently, the percentage of women receiving pain medication during labor tripled. So much for natural childbirth.

Well, it's a little late for me. When I was pregnant with our first child in 1981, my husband and I went to Lamaze classes, just like everybody else we knew, so we'd be prepared for labor. We sat around with other expectant couples and listened to a nurse talk about the history of natural childbirth.

The whole zeitgeist was clear. Childbirth was manageable, normal, natural. It didn't need to be medicalized. All you had to do was breathe correctly and come up with a focal point that usually involved bad macrame, and, voila, you had natural childbirth. You did everything you could to avoid drugs. It was kind of like a marathon, and the women who ran the farthest and fastest would be the best mothers.

We were surrounded by very nice, very earnest people in that room, and the last thing I wanted to do was to make a big public announcement about how *I didn't relate well to pain*. In fact, my original plan had been to plead and beg my doctor for a Caesarian section. But then I heard that they didn't knock you out cold for a C-section, so I was looking for a new plan. Drugs, I thought. Lots of drugs. I wouldn't go to the dentist without drugs. Why should I go through childbirth without them?

Some evenings, in our class, the women lay on the floor and our husbands practiced coaching us. The Dads, the nurse called them. The Dads helped us breathe—*hee, hee, hee, hoooo* —and stay calm and focused. If things got out of whack, the Dads were supposed to massage our abdomens. Effleurage, the nurse called it. The Dads really seemed to like effleurage, but my own, private opinion was that if I were writhing in pain, effleurage would make me file a lawsuit.

Sometimes we heard lectures and saw films about childbirth. Transition was the worst part, obviously. That happened when you were fully dilated and almost ready to deliver. During transition, it was rumored, the Moms veered out of control and started threatening to divorce the Dads for getting them into this whole mess in the first place and screeching for enough pharmaceuticals for an entire professional football team.

By then a lot of the people in our class already were having babies. We got reports on them. A few had used drugs, the nurse told us, shaking her head sadly.

Three or four weeks later, I went into labor, which was fortunate, because I was sure I was about to set a record for the longest pregnancy in the history of the planet. My husband and I drove to the hospital, and I lay on a bed in the birthing room. Four or five hours passed, and it wasn't so bad. We tried some of the breathing exercises, even though we never had gotten around to picking out a focal point. The doctor gave me a shot of something similar to Demerol.

Another hour passed, and I was getting uncomfortable. It must be transition, I figured.

"I would like my epidural, please," I told the nurse.

"Hold on, honey," she said. "You're already past the worst part."

A few minutes later, our eight-pound, two-ounce daughter was born. It was painful, but what the heck? I was high as a runaway kite, overwhelmed and in love with the most beautiful baby I had ever seen. I was woman. I was powerful. I had gone through natural childbirth, sort of. Well, almost.

The next day, while I was lounging around the hospital, I heard a woman bellowing in the birthing room. I shook my head sadly. Some women, I told myself smugly, couldn't handle natural childbirth the way I could. A few hours later I noticed a new baby in the nursery. His head, as I recall it, was roughly the size of the Goodyear blimp. I practically had to be escorted back to my sitz bath after that.

So I ended up having both my children without epidurals, and many of my friends who were devoted to natural childbirth had C-sections and anesthesia. What does that teach you? That labor is different for everybody. It wasn't a marathon. It was the most profound experience of my life—and I'm sure that's true for all mothers, no matter how they give birth.

Somewhere along the childbirth-as-proof-of-character line, it got easy to forget the point. The baby is the point. As a new mother told *The New York Times*, "I think people deliver how they need to deliver." Exactly.

If I Don't Worry, Who Will?

The weather was calm and beautiful, and the sun was beginning to set. My husband and I were sitting on our patio, taking it easy, when I noticed our nine-year-old son playing on top of the garage roof.

On the roof! It was dangerous! He'd fall off and break a leg—if he was lucky! Quick, dial 911!

"Get off that roof immediately!" I yelled. "You're grounded forever!"

"Relax," my husband said. He was using his calm-down-and-get-a-grip voice, which I find particularly irritating. "He's perfectly fine. That's what boys do. They climb things."

Calm down. Don't get excited. Lie down and take deep breaths. That's what my husband always tells me and, frankly, I don't find any of it very helpful when I'm practically in the middle of cardiac arrest.

What does he mean, *relax*? I never relax. (May I quote writer Fran Lebowitz? "There is no such thing as peace of mind," she said. "There is only nervousness and death.")

Besides, I'm the worrier in the family, and I take it all very seriously. I hear a siren and I expect the worst. I take a plane and try to recall if my will is up to date. One of our children gets a fever, and it's probably meningitis. ("Does your neck feel stiff?" I always ask. Stiff necks are a sign of meningitis, although it could be rabies, too. I read that somewhere, years ago. Also rashes. "Do you have a rash anywhere?" I always ask that, too, as long as I'm at it.)

I worry when things are going badly. I really worry when things are going well, because good luck always strikes me as unnerving. I would think I'm pretty weird about all of this, but I have a few friends who worry as much as I do. We're all fairly normal, I like to think, if you don't mind people who are a little neurotic and skittish and jump when they hear loud noises.

Peel back the worry, the fears, the anticipated catastrophes —and what you find is some kind of underlying superstition, some lingering hope, that if we fret and obsess enough, we can avert disaster. In a world where children and adults are slaughtered by terrorists in a city close to ours, we cling to every illusion that we can make ourselves safe. Maybe, if we're vigilant enough, we can keep the monsters away.

Inhibited, fearful, anxious, reactive—that's what a recent article about temperament in *The Atlantic Monthly* called people like me. "Few would wish to be the anxious type," the article says in what I consider to be the understatement of the decade, "but, in an environment filled with predators, or their modern equivalent, having some worriers around is adaptive, at least for the species."

Well, it's always nice to know we're doing something good for the species. It makes us sound like a flock of canaries, sniffing for gases while everyone else mines for ore. Give us relaxation therapy or meditation or aerobics or self-hypnosis, and we might seem calmer—but we're still canaries at heart.

"I'm a real worrier," a friend said a few months ago, when we were talking about her decision on whether to have children. "I wonder if I'd worry even more than I do now if I had children."

I could tell her so much about having children. I could tell her how the diapers would eventually disappear from her life, and so would the bottles and baby food and tantrums and her own exhaustion. They'd all pass, eventually, and everything would get easier.

But worry? That was something that would never leave her, no matter how mature or independent or big her children grew. I hadn't chosen to be a worrier and neither, I'm sure, had she. Somehow, worry had chosen us, and one way or another, it would continue to define us for the rest of our lives.

I didn't say any of this, of course. We just sat there and laughed and talked some more, two canaries sniffing the air for danger.

Mother: The Movie

If you haven't seen the movie *Mother*, you should know that everyone but me thinks it's hilarious. The reviews have been great. The people in the theater were howling with laughter. My husband thought it was wonderful. Albert Brooks, the director and star, is being hailed as a comic genius.

The movie is about a middle-aged writer (Mr. Brooks), whose second marriage breaks up. He realizes that he has problems with women and that he needs to find out why. So he moves back to his childhood home, where his mother (Debbie Reynolds) still lives. He goes home to his mother so he can understand the source of his problems.

I know what my reaction was supposed to be. I should have been identifying with Mr. Brooks. After all, he has this sweetly punishing mother who withholds approval and lavishes bad food and subtle pinpricks of criticism on him. I should have felt all kinds of sympathy for him. I should have laughed at his jokes and his world view.

But I didn't. I couldn't. I identified totally with Debbie Reynolds and the maternal point of view. I knew it was perverse, but I couldn't stop myself.

Throw him out, Debbie, I kept thinking. *You're being way too nice. What does he think he's doing, rearranging your house and criticizing your cheese in the freezer and whining and blaming you for all his problems? Tell him to grow up already!*

The movie went on and on, and everybody but me was practically rolling in the aisles. I was pretty sure I was about to break into a full-body rash. Believe me, it was a very stressful situation for someone who likes to think she has a really great sense of humor.

When you're in a situation like that, when everybody but you is laughing, you can conclude one of two things: Either something is wrong with *them* or something is wrong with *you.* It didn't take me long to choose. I decided everyone else was deeply messed up, especially Albert Brooks. If I had an immature lout of a son like him, I thought, I might change my mind about spanking.

"There are two kinds of mothers," Mr. Brooks has said in interviews. "One is the kind who thinks everything you do is great. This is a movie about the other kind."

Well, of course it's a movie about the other kind. Blame the mother. It figures. Same song, 1082nd verse. Look around in literature and plays and movies and all you find are the destructive mothers who wreck their children's lives. The overbearing mothers. The cold, withdrawn mothers. The alcoholics, the abusers, the addicts. The schizophrenic mothers, the neglectful mothers, the pathologically depressed mothers.

I'm sure that the fact I'm a mother myself might have something to do with my getting very defensive and huffy about all of this. I also know that reasonable, sincere, decent

mothers don't make good theater or books or movies, unless
they try to save their kids' lives and get run over by an express
bus or something.

I know all of that, but I'm still tired of this mother bashing.
I'm so tired of it that I can't even laugh at a comedy about it,
and I seem to have temporarily deep-sixed my sense of humor.
Either that or, as I prefer to think, *Mother* wasn't that hilarious
in the first place, and maybe its attitudes were too much like
real life.

Like my real life. "He has a loose tooth," I said last week. I
was trying to explain to a waiter why my son was only ordering
soup for lunch.

"Mom, please," my son said. "That's embarrassing."

"You remind me of that movie," my husband said, in what I
considered to be a very irritating and unhelpful manner. "You
know, the way Debbie Reynolds was always talking to store
clerks about her son being divorced."

What's wrong with talking a little, I wondered testily.
What's embarrassing about a ten-year-old losing a tooth? Why
don't all you guys grow up and cut your mothers some slack?

The way I see it, there are two kinds of comedies about
mothers.

One is funny.

All of this is about the other kind.

Chapter 3

Marital Relationships

Broken Molars

I wanted to be fair and mature. So I didn't blame my dentist when my tooth broke. I blamed my husband.

After all, it was my husband who'd called me twice when he was in New Zealand for ten days. Both times, he said he was having a great trip. Both times, he reminded me it was summer in the Southern Hemisphere.

Both times, I briefly considered hanging up on him. "I don't want to hear about your trip," I said. "It's raining and cold here. I'm having the worst week of my life."

That was an understatement, as far as I was concerned. My life had gone straight to hell while he was out of town.

Our daughter had hosted her first slumber party, and two of her guests had gone home with their hair spray-painted purple. Our son had gotten sick and vomited all over his G.I. Joe sleeping bag. Our kitten had fallen out of a tree and broken her leg and had to have surgery. Every time I saw her limping around the house, I realized I was watching the money for my spring wardrobe lurch off into the horizon.

The way I saw it, it was my husband's fault. If he'd been here, we could have shared these disasters, kind of like community property. Wasn't that what marriage was all about? Sharing?

We'd have to have a talk when he got back, I decided. This would be a good opportunity for me to learn to express my anger better.

Two days later, when my husband returned, he had jet lag and he looked almost as bad as I did. This gave me a certain satisfaction. "Take a nap," I told him, "and we'll talk about this later."

He wandered off to take a nap, and I sat down to manage my anger in a mature, healthy way that involved eating lots of candy. Just as I was feeling that warm glow of pure sugar, I bit down on something hard. I reached inside my mouth and pulled out a chunk of one of my molars.

Wonderful. Just wonderful. I lay on the floor and thought how much I hated symbolism. To me, this wasn't just a broken tooth; it was a sign that screamed *middle age*. (This was only the beginning, I realized. The rest of my life, clearly, would be spent in constant maintenance and emergency repair.)

The tooth also screamed other things, as well. Things like, *Why were you eating all that candy, anyway?* And, *Boy, you sure are pathetic at handling anger.* I was about to admit that I had no one to blame but myself when it occurred to me that my broken tooth was really my husband's fault. If he hadn't gone to New Zealand, I wouldn't have been forced to eat all that candy. That made me feel even sorrier for myself.

"I don't know why you're complaining so much," said the child I'd nursed through the flu. "I lose teeth all the time, and I don't complain."

"Hang it up, Mom," said the child I'd given the slumber party for. "Why don't you just go ahead and get dentures?"

"You lost a tooth?" said the adult who'd just been to New Zealand. "Ick."

"I'm going to bed," I announced loudly. "I'm in pain and I want to be left alone."

Which everyone did, till the next morning. I woke up to find one child jumping on my stomach and another one turning on the radio full-blast. Beside me, my husband was reaching under my pillow.

"Look!" he said. "Here's a dollar! The tooth fairy must have come for you!" He waved the bill, grinning at me.

Here's a dollar, there's a silver lining, I thought. Maybe it's one of those times when it's all in the attitude. Maybe I'd lost a tooth, but I'd be gaining a crown. It would be gold and shiny, and I could wear it forever. I'd call it my summer wardrobe.

So much for holding grudges and expressing anger. I'd never been any good at it, anyway.

Besides, how could I stay angry at the Tooth Fairy, especially after he'd traveled so far and been away so long?

Ants and Grasshoppers

This is ridiculous.

If I lived in a normal household, someone like me would never be handling money. No way. In fact, a person like me would be kept as far away from finances as possible. It would be against the law for me to handle money.

But no. I don't live in a normal household. My household is ecologically imbalanced, and the natural order has broken down. You see, we don't have the right insect population at our house. We need more ants.

"He's the ant and I'm the grasshopper," my friend Joyce says, talking about her marriage. "That's why he takes care of finances and I don't."

Ants and grasshoppers. That's my point, exactly. Every household needs at least one of each. At Joyce's house, he handles money and she doesn't. He obsesses and she relaxes. He plans and she goes along. He worries and sweats the fine print, and she doesn't even bother to read it.

"I'm a grasshopper, too," I say sulkily. "But I have to handle finances, anyway. That's why we won't be retiring till we're 105."

I'm a grasshopper, too! That's a primal insect scream you hear. The real me is green and gawky and long-legged and careless and slovenly—a madcap heiress grasshopper. I want to hop instead of crawl. I want to let somebody else cross the t's and dot the i's and mind the p's and q's and decimal points.

The trouble is, I'm married to someone who's a bigger grasshopper than I am, and every house needs at least one ant to remember to pay the mortgage and keep the receipts. By sheer and tragic default, I'm the designated ant at my address.

Which is why I spend half my life impersonating an ant—pretending to be an insect I'm not. I'm not the type, but I try. I pay bills on time, and I'm smart enough not to mess with the Internal Revenue Service, and I save some money so I'm not a complete and total dud as a phony ant. I try to walk and talk like an ant. But I'm not a true ant, and eventually it shows.

Take Joyce's household, for example, where a real ant lives. Their finances are in great shape. They actually have a budget and financial plans and projections for the future. I have financial plans, too, but they only last for minutes at a time.

"We're going to keep track of how we spend money over the next month," I announce to the Big Grasshopper. "We need to know exactly where our money is going. That is the first step in coming up with a budget."

He flinches when I say that. We don't use words like "budget" around our house. If anyone ever put disturbing graffiti on our bathroom walls, it wouldn't be a bunch of four-letter words. It would be something like, "Plan for your future." Or, "Can you afford to retire?" Or, "Balance your checkbook." That would be a very cruel thing to do. It would also be pornographic.

"We need a budget," I say loudly, trying to look as fierce and ant-like as possible. "Everyone but us has a budget. We need to get organized. We're going to be keeping track of our money this month."

We tell the children that we're going to record all our expenses this month. They look skeptical, the way they always do when I have a really great idea. They also look a little too long-legged to be ants. As a matter of fact, they look a lot like miniature grasshoppers. It figures.

Our experiment lasts a week, which is a long time for some insects. "Well, at least we've taken the first step," the Big Grasshopper says, looking relieved. "We can multiply this week by four to come up with our monthly expenditures. We've done a lot already."

"We're going to do this next month and we'll stick to it," I say. "We'll do it till we get it right. We need a budget."

The Big Grasshopper tells me to lie down and take deep breaths. He indicates that maybe the word "budget" has upset me unduly. So maybe we shouldn't use it around our house in the future.

Next month, I think. Next month, I'm going to get our family organized. We'll keep track of all our money. We'll come up with a budget. We'll plan for the future. You'll see! Next month, I'll be a great ant, a grand ant. I'll be the queen of the hill.

But that's next month. Right now, this instant, something in me is just dying to hop.

Shopping for China

My husband and I got married twenty-four years ago. We're still vaguely recognizable as the same people in our wedding pictures, especially if the lights are dim and your eyesight is bad.

The everyday china we got as wedding presents, though, looks a lot worse—kind of like it's been fed through a trash compactor. It's been washed, microwaved, heated, cooled, frozen, dropped, bounced, chipped, bashed, and cracked. Even by the low standards of our household, it's time to buy new dishes.

"I've always hated that china," my husband says casually. I stare at one of our surviving dinner plates. It's dark blue, marked by white flowers with yellow centers. I picked it out myself. I can remember how beautiful—how elegant—I thought the pattern was.

What does he mean *he always hated it*?

"I've always loved it," I say, speaking through clenched teeth. "I admit the silverware was a big mistake. But I've always loved our china."

The silver flatware pattern I chose for our wedding was called something awful like "Spanish Dancer's Lace," which probably was grounds for a lawsuit in at least one European country. It had lots of dark, swirly decorations on it, similar to the webs spiders weave when they've taken lots of hallucinogenic drugs. The first time I saw it, I loved it; every time after that, it gave me a cold sore.

Fortunately, though, "Spanish Dancer's Lace" is no longer with us. We sold it several years ago, when the price of silver hit record highs, and paid lots of bills. Sometimes, when I tell people that, they look at me with pity. But they shouldn't. We were perfectly happy to unload it and even happier to make money on it.

But, in the meantime, we still need new china. Late one afternoon my husband and I go to a department store and look at colorful displays of dishes on shiny glass shelves.

"How about this?" I ask, showing him some earth-colored dishes.

He gets a look of polite nausea on his face. It's exactly the same expression he gets when I try to explain to him why I like folk art. "Hmmmm," he says. He touches a white plate with a thin gold rim. "I like this."

"You're kidding," I say. "You actually like that? It looks so delicate." I try to make it clear that this isn't a compliment. Delicate everyday china is for morons.

We move on slowly. We point out what we like. We point out what we don't like. We agree on nothing. We start to glare at each other. We move in different directions.

I begin to wonder what I'd think if I were a sales clerk listening to the two of us and assuming we were picking out our wedding china. I know exactly what I'd think: *Call off the wedding immediately! These two people are completely incompatible about china. Hope they've got a great pre-nup!*

Maybe divorce lawyers cruise the china sections. It might be a good way to drum up business. All you'd have to do is wait till all the screaming and plate-throwing stops.

"What do you think of this?" my husband asks. It's another one of those pale plates with a thin line. Oh, yechh. Spare me.

"I hate it." I don't bother showing him my latest heartthrob, a place setting with strong, vivid colors and a slightly rough texture. Earthy. Vibrant. Kind of like me.

We walk around a little more, but we've lost all our enthusiasm. Finally we give up. We leave the store, empty-handed and testy.

On the way back, we insult each other and laugh, driving through the dark streets toward home. "I guess I never realized what terrible taste you have," my husband says.

"You need an aesthetics transplant," I tell him.

So there we are. Our silverware has been hocked and melted down, and our everyday china is suffering a major breakdown, and we can't agree on even a new pattern for salad plates.

But twenty-four years later, I still have more fun with my husband than anyone else I know—even if the guy does have wretched taste in china. Some patterns, I like to think, are more important than others.

———— 🍎 ————

Ulysses S. Grant Sends His Regrets

The minute I heard about Laura Doyle's new book, *The Surrendered Wife: A Practical Guide to Finding Intimacy, Passion and Peace with Your Man*, I knew I had to try it. It sounded so easy! All you had to do was say to your husband "whatever you think" every time he came up with a brilliant idea like fixing the plumbing in your house. Then, after he'd managed to flood the place like a rice paddy, you didn't criticize him.

You also didn't criticize him when he took the wrong freeway exit and ended up in another country, or when he forgot to pay your phone bill and you got disconnected. This is because you should allow him to be in charge of masculine things like driving and handling finances and giving you an allowance, which you should always be very grateful for.

I know, I know. So there were a few drawbacks. But the rewards looked great. Doyle lists a number of frenzied testimonials about how your husband will want to "delight" and provide for you, the newly surrendered woman. Take Gina, for example. Since she turned over finances to her husband, she has no earthly idea what kind of salary he earns; all she knows is that she's the beneficiary of much more disposable income than she was before. (Much more disposable income? Either Gina's surrendered a few dozen I.Q. points or she's never watched *The Sopranos*.)

But anyway, I talked to my friends Betsy and Becky and we decided we'd all spend the rest of the day surrendering to our husbands and seeing whether our marriages instantly improved. (Sure, the book recommended six months before you leveled with your husband, but who has that kind of time these days?)

"Do you ever think you'd like to handle our finances again?" I asked my husband.

"Are you crazy?" he said. He looked panicked, like he needed the Heimlich maneuver or something.

"But you're so much better at things like that than I am," I said. If you think this was an easy line to deliver with a straight face, you would be wrong. I'm pretty sure I'm going to be up for one of the lesser Academy Awards next year for that little performance.

"Don't you remember what happened the last time I handled our money?" he asked.

Well, of course I did. He'd loudly congratulated himself on how much money we still had at the end of the month. A few days later he noticed that our newfound affluence came from forgetting to pay the mortgage that month. I'd been too critical at the time, I suppose, which Doyle says is a very typical problem in most marriages. My husband needed to build up his self-esteem again by handling our finances. The trouble is, my husband already had a lot of self-esteem. I wasn't sure he needed more.

But I kept at it. We went to a dinner party that night, and I kept trying to surrender to my husband. Unfortunately, we were in different rooms most of the evening, and it's very hard to surrender to someone who's not in the same room. (What if Grant hadn't shown up at Appomattox?) *Surrender, surrender,* I went around telling myself. *Remember Gina and all her disposable income.*

"It didn't work," Betsy said the next morning. "I couldn't handle that surrender stuff. So I just went straight on to the part of the book I liked: Naming my desires."

That was a part of the book I'd especially liked, too. You were supposed to tell your husband what you wanted, and since he was so deliriously giddy about your being a surrendered wife and everything, he would immediately go out and get everything for you. How would he pay for it? Well, finances were his problem, not yours.

"I told him I wanted to go to Florence," Betsy continued. "Maybe I should have stopped there. But I didn't. I told him I also wanted new furniture and a new car. He seemed kind of shocked by the whole thing."

"That's because you've been so deprived all these years," I said. Personally, though, I was pretty sure Betsy had blown it. If she'd followed the book and all its "whatever you think" rules, she'd probably be strolling on the Ponte Vecchio right now.

Then I talked to Becky, who very proudly reported she'd gone to the mall with her husband without mentioning his bermuda shorts stained with shrimp taco sauce even once. Then, after they got home, she'd told him that she'd greet him all bound up in Saran wrap the following night.

"He said, What for?" Becky revealed. "He thought it was some kind of new cellulite treatment."

At last report, Betsy still hasn't gone to Florence, Becky's husband is still wearing the same shrimp taco-stained shorts, and she never did get out the Saran wrap, and my husband's relieved to know he doesn't have to handle our money, and I don't need a lobotomy for my recent personality change.

So there you are. If this is what happens when you surrender, I want a refund. Maybe I'll call Laura Doyle and ask her advice.

But what if her husband forgot to pay the phone bill last month? Now, that would be some kind of great, cosmic justice. If you had to disconnect one woman, she would be the one.

———— ĕ ————

My Husband, the Psychologist

You can get used to any kind of situation and start thinking it's normal if you're around it long enough. That's what I was thinking at my husband's fiftieth birthday party, when our daughter was toasting him.

She talked about growing up in a household where her father once wore a pair of enormous electronic ears that made him look like Mickey Mouse on growth hormones. She mentioned how her father would always tell her and her younger brother to write about any problems they had. (This is based on his psychological research showing that writing about emotions and traumas improves mental and physical health. But try telling that to our kids. "I'm sick of writing about things!" one or both of them would routinely howl in answer. "Stop telling me to write! It doesn't do any good!") She spoke about how he carried a microphone to soccer games and city streets to record snatches of conversation so he could analyze how people talk to one another.

Oh, yeah, I thought. *Right. If you were a total stranger hearing all these stories, you'd think the guy being described was kind of odd.*

I watched my husband, who was beaming proudly and wet-eyed as our daughter finished her toast. I've now been around him for so many years, I realized, that I don't always notice how unusual he is. I'm used to him, kind of.

I was there, close to the beginning of his career as a psychologist, when he played his clarinet in the London underground and a friend would occasionally toss change in the cup by his feet. It was a modeling experiment, he told me, designed to influence others to give, too. I think he also tried to explain that to the official who escorted him out of the underground, along with his clarinet, his tin cup, and his botched experiment.

I was there, too, when he and I went to a party thrown by a high-ticket law firm more than twenty years ago. Most of the people we were next to were law students like me, hovering around an important partner in the firm who was asking us about ourselves, one by one. When he got to my husband, my husband replied that he was a graduate student in psychology, not a law student. For some reason, the partner began to make fun of him. "Where's your white coat?" he asked. "Where's your rat? Ha, ha, ha." Ha, ha, ha, the other law students echoed nervously.

I watched my husband first try to be polite (after all, we were there because of me), then flush with anger and abruptly give up the struggle. "You know what?" he told the partner. "You're right. Psychologists do funny things. You know that right this minute, I can see directly into you? I can read your mind." He stared directly at the partner, who turned sheet white and almost spilled his drink. The partner mumbled some kind of excuse and staggered away from the group. "I don't think you'll be getting any offers from that firm," my husband whispered, and what do you know, he was right.

The years passed, and I was there when he hauled a machine around to test everyone's blood pressure in bars. When he sent students out to find that Mickey Gilley was right and yes, indeed, "The Girls All Get Prettier at Closing Time." When he raced to Mount St. Helens after it blew, studied physical and emotional reactions to the San Francisco earthquake, the Gulf War, the Kennedy assassination, and Princess Diana's death. Name a mishap, and he's mildly interested. Name a full-blown disaster, and he's there.

Sure, I know it sounds kind of strange, but as I said, I'm used to it. For one thing, he earns his living as an academic psychologist—teaching, doing research, consulting, giving talks. He works constantly, but this isn't normal work he does. More than anything, he follows his own interests and instincts.

Sometimes it works and sometimes it doesn't. Sometimes I follow him and sometimes I don't.

A few years ago he talked me into a detour to Albania, against my own more cautious nature. "It's the fast way to get from Italy to Greece," he kept telling me. "It's practically a short cut." No matter who tried to talk him out of it—half the psychologists in Italy, as far as I could tell—he was intent on going. So what if everyone insisted we were crazy or naïve or stupid or all three? "Those people haven't even been to Albania," he pointed out. "What do they know about it?"

"Why are you going to Albania?" the stewardess on the ship between Italy and Albania asked us. (We had already been bumped up to VIP class, since we were the only passengers on the boat who weren't being deported back to Albania. It was that kind of ship.)

"Because it sounds interesting," my husband said, sensing another meddling West European who didn't know what she was talking about. "Where are *you* from, anyway?"

"Albania," she said.

"Oh," he muttered quietly.

Beginning then and for the next two days, I frequently thought about strangling him for his enduring curiosity and love of adventure. I thought about it every time we passed one of the hundreds of thousands of bunkers in the Albanian hills that had been purchased by a paranoid former leader from the Chinese. Every time we passed gangly groups of teenage soldiers armed with machine guns and testosterone. Every time we saw one of the many roadside shrines for people who'd been hauled out of their cars and summarily executed after the country's economy collapsed in a pyramid scheme the year before.

But I didn't. I realized how, in spite of everything, we travel light and we travel well together. If I hadn't been with my husband, the world I've seen would have been very different—more organized and predictable, but not nearly as much fun. Happy Father's Day to the most interesting person I've ever known.

Sunday Brunches

We were civilized then. The flowers were fresh and the tablecloth was starched and snowy and voices hovered at a low murmur above the soft, classical music. Almost every Sunday noon in the early years of our marriage, that's where you'd find my husband and me, in a nice, peaceful restaurant, eating contentedly, talking quietly, easing luxuriously into another new week.

The years passed, and we started having babies. We weren't so civilized by then. Four years apart, our two babies had lots of personality. They liked to gurgle loudly and smear oatmeal all over their little bald heads and bang their spoons on the metal highchair trays like they were auditioning to play bass drum in the marching band. As long as someone in our house was in diapers, we didn't even think about going out for Sunday brunch at nice, peaceful restaurants any longer. We weren't into that kind of public humiliation.

And what do you mean, *easing luxuriously into another new week*? Get real. Sundays, with babies and toddlers, my husband and I lurched and skidded and sprawled into new weeks, mopping up milk and orange juice and more unsavory spills, surviving for months and years without ever finishing a sentence or a conversation or a meal. Easing luxuriously was what we called it when somebody didn't have pink eye or diaper rash or a major stomach virus. Other people had weeks like that, maybe; we didn't.

More years passed, and we began to go out again on Sunday mornings—the four of us. At first we ventured out cautiously, like storm victims poking their way out of a tornado shelter after the big one has hit. If a restaurant was shabby and inexpensive and loud, it was playing our new, nonclassical song: Any place that low-rent, we always figured, had to be child-friendly. So what if one or both of our children were in a ketchup-on-everything stage? Or if they told their usual see-food joke by opening their full mouths? We came and went quickly in those days, leaving shredded napkins, empty ketchup bottles, and big tips behind us.

Time throttled on, and our children announced that they, too, loved to eat out. Frequently. From the time they were barely out of high chairs and booster seats, they were already eerily adept at asking waitresses and waiters for the check.

Worse, they had strong opinions about everything culinary, which they often had brawls about in the back seat of the car.

"Pizza!"

"I'm tired of pizza! I want Tex-Mex!"

"What's wrong with Asian food?"

"Shut up."

"We're not supposed to say shut up. Mom!"

"Shut up, shut up, shut up."

They quickly (too quickly) discovered they both liked sushi, which my husband and I actually thought was kind of cute at first. Now, we just think it's expensive. Beyond their strong opinions about food (and assuming we can ever agree on a place to go to brunch without spilling blood, for crying out loud), our now-teenage daughter and son also haul loud, stubborn, a la carte opinions about everything from politics to sports to musical groups to family concerns to the table on Sundays.

"I hate the book I'm reading."

"We have to get back to watch the Cowboys play."

"Mom, hurry up."

"Everybody I know gets a bigger allowance than I do."

"Why do I have to have a curfew?"

"I'm going to be president when I grow up."

"Can we get the new Cake CD?"

"Mom, you're taking too long."

"We're ready for our check, please."

Our Sunday brunches are livelier, the talk is louder, the checks have skyrocketed, and if there's classical music playing in the background, we still can't hear it. But we've gotten used to it; we've come to love it. Somewhere along the way, we finally figured out that family traditions have to be flexible to survive.

Family traditions—and families themselves. One of our strongest voices is going off to college this month. College! We can't believe it. She's almost the age her father and I were when we began our Sunday brunch tradition.

I think back to that time and wonder. Did we really like it when it was that quiet? Will we like it when it's quiet once again?

Will we? I ask my husband.

He winks at me and laughs. "Of course we will," he says. "We'll get used to it again." In the background, I could swear I hear the soft music beginning.

Chapter 4

Men and Women, Women and Men

Fireworks

Don't think for one minute that I'm going to get into the psychosexual aspects of fireworks. No way. No cheap cracks about Freud or testosterone or the symbolism of explosions or the immaturity of men. I'm above all that.

All I know is, after the first explosion echoed from our back yard four years ago, every man and boy in our neighborhood came running. It was our first Fourth of July in our new house and, as usual, my husband was exploding something.

"I'm surprised," the woman across the street said to me. "You're husband seems so mild-mannered."

"Ha," I said.

She and I were huddled inside our house, which is where I stay every Fourth of July. It's been this way for years, ever since my husband and I discovered we have a difference of opinion about explosives.

"That's sick," I used to tell him at the top of my lungs. "Didn't you ever read *Follow My Leader* when you were a kid?" I had. It was a book about a boy who had been blinded when a neighborhood gang threw a firecracker in his face. "Leader," I always added ominously, "was the name of his guide dog."

The years passed, and I still hated fireworks and my husband still loved them. We reached an uneasy truce. It was just one day a year, I reasoned. At least it was predictable. If he wanted to risk his neck every Fourth of July, I finally agreed, it was his own business. It was a marital compromise, like cold feet and dirty clothes.

As for me, I'd spend the whole day inside, where it was safe. I'd keep the children away from the windows, make sure my husband's life insurance policy was up to date, stick cotton in my ears, and earn bonus points for martyrdom. All of which worked for a few years.

But now, as I peered out the window, I realized my problem had just gotten bigger. There were almost twenty men and boys in our back yard, helping my husband make his own fireworks. This is a process my husband insists is "creative."

The hours passed, and the gang in our back yard exploded a homemade pipe bomb, bottle rockets, and a whole ensemble of firecrackers. Fingers, toes, arms, and legs were all intact, along with other appendages, and spirits were high. My husband, who smelled strongly of gunpowder, said it had been the best Fourth of July of his life. I told him to take a bath and talk to me in the morning, when there was a better chance I'd be speaking to him.

Well, so much for marital compromises. Every year since then, the Fourth has gotten bigger and rowdier in our neighborhood. This growing group of middle-aged men and their wide-eyed sons have lit up the skies and shattered the quiet of hot, calm July afternoons. Occasionally, the police have come and gone, never suspecting that this group of respectable-looking men with advanced degrees and shiny bifocals could be disturbing the peace.

For the most part, I don't fight it. I've got other, more important battles to wage. And, as I said, I don't want to get into the psychosexual aspects of this.

But wait a minute. What do I mean, *I don't want to get into it*? Once a year, once in my lifetime, why not? What the hell.

Forget campfires, drum-beating, Iron John, myths and tears as the great male-bonding experiences of our time.

In my neighborhood, men bond with fireworks and loud noises, gunpowder, and derring-do. It's a limited war where they take no prisoners, and they're all four-star generals for a day. I have no idea why the men I know act this way, and it's not getting any clearer with age. Maybe the differences lie in nature and/or nurture, pink or blue blankets at birth, or in the chromosomes and the mysteries of XX and XY.

Who can say? All I know is, for one day a year, I've agreed that it's not mine to question Y.

———— 🍎 ————

The Laws of the Jungle

I've now been the mother of a son for eight years, and I still don't get it. I still don't understand boys.

Maybe it's my background. I grew up without brothers, and the man I know best—my husband—was pretty much fully formed by the time I met him. No assembly was required, even though, God knows I've tried. ("Why can't we drink out of the milk carton? Dad does it and you never say anything," my two children like to complain. "I'm not Dad's mother," I tell them. "I'm not in charge of his manners. I'm in charge of yours." I say it automatically now. That's what happens when you repeat yourself several thousand times a day.)

But anyway, boys. They fascinate me and they puzzle me. They're like a foreign country, and I don't speak the language. I can visit, but I don't belong.

"Are your feelings hurt?" I ask my son. "How do you feel?" (This is so I can teach him to be emotionally expressive. Also sensitive, caring, and vulnerable. His wife is going to thank me someday.)

"I don't know," he says. Or, "I forgot."

I watch him and his friends tussle like puppies. Everything's action, everything's physical, and they end up sprawling on the floor. Outside, they play soccer and baseball and touch football that always turns to tackle, no matter how often I shriek dementedly from the sidelines that tackling isn't allowed at our house.

All of this—and I'm from the generation that said we were going to rear our sons and daughters to be the same. Differences were environmental, we said. We were going to make our sons sensitive and our daughters assertive, and maybe we've succeeded to some degree. Maybe, but I'm not sure. Lately, I'm not even sure what "success" is.

I'm sure that unconsciously and in spite of ourselves, we rear boys and girls differently and then we send them out into a world that treats them even more differently. But I'm not convinced that the differences between the sexes are purely environmental.

All I know is that I have one child who's been to the emergency room twice, chipped three teeth, had a concussion, makes car noises, likes to play with stuffed animals by body-slamming them, wants to grow up to be a professional wrestler—and it isn't my daughter I'm talking about. Call it anecdotal evidence, but I live with these anecdotes.

This same child has telephone conversations that continue to amaze me—"*Hello. Yeah. Yeah. Yeah. Bye.*" (click)—that no self-respecting female over the age of two would dream of calling a conversation.

Watching him grow up, I see this boy's world unfold, and it amuses, intrigues, and mystifies me. I understand my daughter fairly well; I'm learning about my son, and sometimes I'm not sure I'm passing the course.

Two months ago, when an older boy took one of my son's toys and didn't return it, I scolded the older child over the phone. My husband was appalled.

"You've just broken one of the laws of the jungle when it comes to boys," he said, quietly horrified. "You're never supposed to interfere."

Another day, another mistake, I thought; I'm still learning about boys. I filed it away with my other lessons (e.g., *Don't be too mushy! Don't kiss him in front of his friends! Don't be overprotective!*). Then I thought about it more and realized my husband was wrong.

Maybe he and my son know all about this male world, and maybe I have a lot to learn. But I know something about the law of the jungle, guys: If you mess with a mother animal and her young, you'll get your head bitten off.

Men and Machines and the Women Who Love Them

We have a new ceiling fan in our bedroom, which is fine. We also have a new remote control to operate it, which isn't fine.

"Do you want the fan to go faster?" my husband asks. He's clutching the remote control, and he looks ecstatic. He always looks that way around new machines, especially when they come with remote controls. "Or we can reverse the direction, if you like."

Everything is fine, I tell him.

"Do you think the lights are too bright?" he asks eagerly. "I can dim them, too."

No, I don't want the lights dimmed. No, I don't want the fan reversed. No, I don't want any more remote controls or pushy new machines in my life. And no, I certainly don't want to cast aspersions on any particular sex, but the men in my life are driving me crazy with all their new technology. I think I'm going to join a nineteenth-century agrarian commune or something.

"Can I turn on the fireplace?" our son asks every day after school. The temperature's 90 and the humidity's higher. But he wants to turn on the gas fireplace because it has a remote control, too. My son and my husband practically get misty-eyed when they talk about it.

"It's just like the fireplace on *Clueless*," my husband says. "Don't you remember that great scene?"

No, I say sulkily. I remember the clothes, the hairstyles, and the plot in *Clueless*. But I have no memory whatsoever of a remote-controlled fireplace. My husband acts as if that was the pivotal scene of the whole movie and I'm missing the point.

Well, I haven't missed the point. It's just that I have a better point, and I'm pretty sure Jane Austen would back me up on it. I think that if you want a fire, you should have to chop wood and haul it in and light it yourself and blow on it till your face turns blue. (In my nineteenth-century agrarian commune, this would be someone else's job.)

As a matter of fact, I don't like remote-controlled anything. I'm too tactile for that. I like things and people I can touch. I don't want to read cyberbooks, either; I want real ones.

I also don't like having all this new machinery pushed on me by my husband, even if it isn't remote-controlled. I have to take a long time to bond with a machine. It took me three years to learn to trust my last computer, which my husband says is a "sad commentary." (When we bought the computer, he said it was a work of art. Since last year, he's been referring to it as "that piece of junk in your office." In the computer age, loyalty has a shorter shelf life than a ripe banana.)

My husband reminds me that it's the '90s and I need a computer that moves quickly. As a matter of fact, he's embarrassed about how ancient my computer is. I tell him that maybe I like an older, slower computer so I can identify with it.

But last week my husband got a brand-new computer, and he gave me his "old" 1996 model. It certainly is fast, if you like that kind of thing. It also makes little noises, like chords, when you make a mistake. It gives you messages, too, like you're some kind of idiot, so you know when you can turn it off. But at least it doesn't talk to me. I hate machines that talk to me.

"Isn't it wonderful?" my husband says.

He looks so happy that I tell him, yes, I like the computer. Really, it's just great. To think of all those milliseconds I've wasted in the past, just waiting for my old computer and modem to work, I say.

"I told you you'd love it," he says, ignoring my tone.

As I said, I certainly don't want to cast aspersions on males. I'm sure there are millions of men who hate new technology and remote controls and millions of women who love them (the machines, I mean). But at our house, the men worship high technology, automatic fires, and channel surfing, and I tolerate them on my better days.

Which is precisely the kind of day I wasn't having last week, when the son of one of the men working on our house came inside to get a drink of water. He's in middle school, he said, but he helps his father in the late afternoons. He walked around the house and told me how much better it looked after weeks of work.

I smiled and nodded and started to point out how nice the new cabinets and floors looked. But then I noticed he was staring at something behind me.

"Oh, wow," he breathed. "Oh, *wow*. Is that a remote-controlled fireplace?"

His expression, I swear to you, was rapt.

Chick Flicks: Crying Is Its Own Reward

Last year I went to a psychology conference and listened to several presentations. It was an international group of Americans and Europeans, and all the accents, ideologies, and World Cup soccer allegiances were often snarled and confusing.

One morning a psychologist from Holland presented findings about his research on when men and women cry. "One thing I don't understand," he said near the end of his presentation, "is women's idea that there is such a thing as a good cry. Some of them say they like to go to sad movies so they can have a good cry. I'm not sure what a good cry is."

He turned to the group and shrugged his shoulders helplessly. I looked around the circle of participants, from face to face, and the pattern was clear. No matter what their nationality, the men appeared as perplexed as the Dutch psychologist, and the women looked amazed and a little scornful.

How could these guys not understand the idea of a good cry? What was wrong with them, anyway?

That's what I thought about when the movie *One True Thing* came to town. Based on Anna Quindlen's second novel, it's the story of a young woman returning home to care for her mother, who's dying from cancer. I read that it was a tearjerker packed with wrenching emotions, insights, and great acting. There were no car chases, runaway missiles, explosions, or mangled bodies. "Time to gather," I told my friend, Betsy. "It's a chick flick."

Believe me, I didn't mention the movie to my husband or twelve-year-old son. After years of being rejected by them, I've finally gotten the hint. The last straw came a few years ago when the new version of *Little Women* was released, and I tried to talk my son into going to it with me when my husband was out of town.

"What's it about?" he asked suspiciously.

I told him it was the story of a family during the Civil War.

"Do you see anybody get killed in the war?" he said. "Are there any battle scenes?"

Well, no, I said, but one of the characters *does* die and—

"Then what's the point?" he wanted to know.

I never figured out the answer to that one. Either you understood or you didn't. So my daughter and I went to the movie, and we cried and had a wonderful time. Give me an old-fashioned, sentimental film like that—or *The Way We Were* or *Old Yeller* or *Two for the Road*—and I'll be writhing in the aisles, sobbing. If that's not rewarding, if that's not a great time, then what is?

Still, it's one of those sharply defined moments when I realize I don't understand the man and boy in my life, and they don't understand me. It's like the time I watched my son skate to the park with a friend to see if a dead squirrel was still lying there, squashed, on the sidewalk. Or when he told me about the ideal civilization he and two classmates were creating for a project.

"We use the death penalty a lot," he told me. "Also, if someone lies, we cut off his legs."

"What about the other kids who're working with you?" I asked. "Are they boys, too?"

"What do you think?" he says.

What do I think? Oh, I don't know. I think I'm not about to waste my time talking to either of these two testosterone cases about seeing *One True Thing*. It's a school night when I go, and my daughter is too busy with homework to come. So Betsy and I go, along with Pat and Marian. Marian says she knows she won't cry, as long as animals don't get hurt. Later Betsy says she didn't cry as much as she'd expected.

But Pat and I sit there, grabbing tissues and weeping. When the movie's over, we stagger toward the door. "Nobody," I tell Pat, "but *nobody* can die as well as Meryl Streep."

"How was it?" my family asks when I get back. I look at their three expectant faces.

"Great," I say. "It was a good movie, and I cried a lot."

Three expectant faces, and only one gazes back at me knowingly. "I wish I could have gone," she says.

Whipped Cream Rules

When the *Three Stooges* came on TV, her husband and two sons would excitedly lock themselves in the den to watch. They wouldn't let her come in the room till "the girl" on the *Three Stooges* made her entrance.

"Each one of them was a different stooge," Pamela recalls. "I never understood it, but it was very important to them—*which stooge they were*. I never could tell the difference, could you?"

Which stooge they were? That was important?

I used to laugh hysterically when I heard stories like that. What a riot. They were always being told by my friends like Pamela, who were completely outnumbered by the males in their households. To hear them talk, they were barely afloat in a river of can-crushing, monosyllables, movies with fiery car chases instead of heartbreak, fireworks, red meat, and jokes about flatulence.

I used to laugh. But now I've stopped.

Ever since our daughter went off to college, our household has been out of whack. For years we'd had a gender-balanced house, but now I have to live alone with my two favorite XY cases—my husband and son. I'm still getting used to it.

I tell my husband, for example, that our son is in the living room watching something called *Great Car Wrecks of 2000* on TV. I expect him to shake his head sadly, the way I am. Instead, I notice, he looks interested.

I return from a trip to a colder climate with a taste for Irish coffee. We already have the ingredients, except for whipped cream, which I go to the store to buy. The whipped cream disappears quickly. Suspiciously quickly. I buy more whipped cream before I notice what's going on. Both the guys I live with are bolting to the refrigerator morning, noon, and night, grabbing the can of whipped cream and spraying a white cloud into their mouths.

"Hey, it doesn't mess up any dishes, and you're always griping about dishes," my husband protests. "You should try it sometime before you criticize it. It makes a great breakfast."

The three of us return to the grocery store. "I'm buying two whipped creams this time," I tell them. We head off into three different directions. A few minutes later, as I'm lingering in front of the dairy section, I hear something muffled over the intercom. Then it gets louder, echoing through the store, bouncing off the milk cartons.

"Ruth Pennebaker! Ruth Pennebaker! Please step up to the register! Your husband and son are waiting for you! RUTH PENNEBAKER!"

After forcibly separating my husband from the intercom system, we leave. "Hey, the checkout kid said it was OK if I made an announcement," my husband chortles on the way home. "He told me I was pretty good at it, too."

"You should have seen your face," our son says. "You looked so embarrassed!"

We arrive home, and I explain the new whipped cream rules. "I bought two," I tell my husband and son. "One is mine and one is yours. Got it? I'm putting a curse on mine. Whoever uses it will lose a vital part of his anatomy."

I write my initials on my whipped cream canister, then pen a warning in a black marker: "Sure, it's good—but is it worth your manhood???"

"You told them that?" asks my friend Betsy, who lives with her husband and two sons. She looks amazed. "I can't believe you said that. Wow."

I nod. "They haven't messed with my whipped cream since then."

A few days later Betsy reports she's told my whipped cream saga to her husband, Mark, and sons, Aaron and James. They loved it, she says. They thought it was one of the funniest stories they ever heard.

For a few minutes, I feel smug. Ecstatic. Brilliant, even.

We're winning the battle of the sexes, I gloat silently. Finally! I can just feel it. Estrogen power! Rightful female dominance! The refrigerator is ours!

For just a few minutes, as I say. That's before Betsy goes on to correct my mistaken impression. "Oh, they didn't care about that stuff about their manhood," she says. "They didn't even notice that. They were just so pleased to hear you could squirt whipped cream directly into your mouth. They'd never thought of that."

They had never thought of that and now, thanks to me, they have. What kind of stooge am I? I don't know. I still get them all confused. I think I'll just be "the girl," like Pamela.

Splitting Votes

As the country lurches toward the 2000 presidential election, political and psychological experts are reporting an alarming increase in tension and violent outbursts among couples who are supporting different presidential candidates. "We haven't seen this kind of marital discord since the Kennedy-Nixon election in 1960," said one pundit, who pleaded not to be identified, since his wife had recently "gone ballistic" over his decision to vote Republican.

"You won't believe the stories I've been hearing," the man said. "Screaming matches over hors d'oeuvres at Le Cirque. Spilled drinks. Chocolate mousses smashed in the other person's face. At those prices, too! You could spend your whole tax cut at that restaurant and still go home hungry. This whole thing has gotten out of hand."

Most recently, according to a story making the rounds in Manhattan and Washington circles, a prominent Georgetown wife is said to have flung a baguette at her husband when he revealed he "didn't give a hang about that whole Supreme Court thing, if you want to know the truth, you overgrown bimbo." Sources close to the battling couple, who have each hired attorneys, refused to verify whether the baguette in question was made by Fendi or a local baker.

As the anecdotal reports of nationwide marital strife continue to mount, social scientists say the warning signs indicate a new and dangerous epidemic—or, even worse, a *syndrome*—may be in the making.

"It's one of the perils of living in a democracy—and being married," chuckled Dr. H. Bradford Foote, who holds the B.F. Skinner Memorial Chair of Behaviorism, Truth and Rodent Studies at Tri-Cities Community College in Michigan's Upper Peninsula (TCCCMUP). "It makes you think that maybe we shouldn't have given women the right to vote," he added jokingly.

Dr. Foote and his wife, Dr. Fiona Foote-Tranchina, a professor of women's studies and gender oppression and inequity at TCCCMUP, are co-authors of the new best-selling book *Splitting Votes Without Splitting Heirs (or Splitting Up)!* The book was inspired by the couple's own difficulties in resolving their political differences, the two academicians recently revealed.

Interviewed over a savory white wine at their elegant, multilevel home overlooking one of the Great Lakes, Dr. Foote and Dr. Foote-Tranchina laughingly recalled the early, onerous years of what they described as their now "picture-perfect" marriage.

"It was kind of upsetting at first," admitted Dr. Foote-Tranchina, slinging back her second glass of wine while her husband pried open a fresh bottle. "I mean, I kept thinking, Jeez, Louise, have I married a total jerkface neanderthal? But then I realized that this was an opportunity for us to grow as a couple by accepting each other's divergent beliefs.

"You know what I mean? It's back to all that 1970s *I'm OK, You're OK* business. When somebody gets the idea that, yeah, well, *I'm OK, You're a Boneheaded Fascist*, then a marriage can really go down the tubes. I mean, even when you're married to a boneheaded fascist, you shouldn't go around saying things like that."

"We've learned to fight fair," chimed in Dr. Foote, blowing his wife a kiss and accidentally spilling most of his wine on her shoes. "We've put our marriage in a lock box. We're uniters, not dividers."

Among their many tips for positive marital vote splitting, the two social scientists suggest:

- Refraining from unproductive name-calling, such as "tree-huggers," "right-wing scum" and "pink-o";

- Refusing to issue interpersonal threats or ultimatums, such as "You're going to be sleeping on the couch for the next four years, you goose-stepping cretin" when tempers are high;

- Using gentle humor to defuse potentially angry exchanges—with an emphasis on the gentle.

BAD EXAMPLE OF GENTLE HUMOR:

"Go ahead and drill the whole darned Arctic if you want, you jackbooted greedheads."

BETTER EXAMPLE OF GENTLE HUMOR:

"Oh, cupcake, even though your candidate's going to empty our pockets with all his spend-spend-spend, wild, liberal, degenerate, stick-it-to-the-rich plans, it doesn't matter. We'll still have each other in the poor house."

"It's really about respecting your partner," said Dr. Foote-Tranchina. "Brad has the right to his opinions, even though they're disgusting and vile and reactionary. I mean, what does this guy know about human beings or politics? He studies rats all the time. I guess that's why he feels so comfortable around Republicans."

Dr. Foote, who was busily cleaning up the pate de foie gras his wife had playfully smeared on his tie during an earlier riposte, chuckled fondly. "Women get suffrage and men suffer," he said. "Ha, ha, ha."

"Stick it in your lock box," his wife said, with gentle humor.

Chapter 5

Holidays, Seasons, and Other Special Occasions

The Science of Love

Hooray! It's Valentine's Day, one of Ms. Pennebaker's favorite holidays. She's sure that all you husbands and boyfriends out there have already flooded your significant others with flowers, candy, jewelry, and silk negligees. Of course you have!

To make this day even better, Ms. P wants to share some groundbreaking scientific findings with all you men. This is news that will make your household as romantic as Valentine's Day the year around!

Scientists have discovered that the sight of men doing housework is an aphrodisiac for women.

Yes, it's true! The vision of a man scrubbing the floors is even more of a turn-on than a pound of Belgian chocolates or cheap fantasies about Joseph Fiennes writing a sonnet for you. There's scientific proof.

Just two days ago Ms. P talked at length with the brilliant researcher behind those findings, Dr. Fiona Foote-Tranchina. She reached Dr. F-T at her home in the Tri-Cities area of Michigan.

"I'm watching my husband right now—vacuuming the living room," Dr. F-T said. "I never knew it could be this way. We're on our second honeymoon. I can't—*Brad, sweetheart, you missed a spot over there. That's good—under the couch. No, on the right side! That's it, dumpling!*—Oops, where was I? Oh, yes. I can't keep my hands off him. What a rush!"

Dr. F-T said the genesis of her highly original research came from her girlhood crush on Mr. Clean. "Mr. Clean was so—*so masculine*," she said. "He looked just like Yul Brynner, except he cleaned houses. I used to fantasize that Mr. Clean would come to my house and—*Oh, Brad, sweetheart, angel! This carpet never has looked better. It looks so soft. I wonder if we could…*"

After that, the conversation came to an abrupt halt because of Dr. F-T's increased panting and gasping for breath. By this time, Ms. P was a little tired of Dr. F-T's Meg-Ryan-in-a-delicatessen impression, anyway. So, after being on hold for an hour, she hung up.

Fortunately, Ms. P already felt sufficiently conversant with Dr. F-T's research to be able to offer advice to men across the country, who clearly need to know more about this revolutionary and titillating work. Just ask, and she'll answer.

Dear Ms. P: Is there any kind of housework that turns women on the most?—Mike M. in University Park

Dear Mike: You have to experiment with many different kinds of chores before you find out what does the trick. Start with the kitchen. It's impossible to resist a man who turns a health department violation into something sparkling and pristine. Ms. P speaks from limited experience on this one, however. She would like much more experience. Is anybody listening?

Dear Ms. P: I did the dishes three times last week, but my wife got a headache every night. What's wrong? Was it me? Or the detergent?—Harry S. in Carrollton

Dear Harry: Ms. P is afraid you've left out some very important details. Did your wife have to nag you to do the dishes? Dr. F-T's research shows that housework done under duress doesn't have the desired aphrodisiac effect. In fact, it appears only to increase a woman's desire to throw large objects, such as lounge chairs, 1957 Chevrolets, and grand pianos, at all men within a 50-yard radius.

So cut out your complaining, Harry. Do the dishes this week without being reminded, and you'll have a tigress on your hands.

Dear Ms. P: What should I wear while I'm doing housework? —Randy X. in Fort Worth

Dear Randy: Nothing in particular.

Dear Ms. P: My wife tells me that she prefers to do housework herself. What can I do? I'm ready to clean right now! Should I go to somebody else's house?—Puzzled, but Extremely Eager in Arlington

Dear Puzzled: Ms. P is as tolerant and nonjudgmental as the next person. But, to be blunt, she wonders what kind of fruitcake you're married to. Marital counseling may be helpful to find out why your wife has such big problems.

In the meantime, whatever you do, don't try to clean someone else's house. You'd be playing with fire.

Dear Ms. P: I can't believe the effect housework has on my wife! I'm cleaning the windows, walls, floors—everything! Whoa, baby! I wish I'd known about this years ago. I would write more, but I just finished cleaning the den, and my wife wants to "talk" to me. Whooppee! You wouldn't believe the "conversations" we've been having recently.—Joe in Mesquite.

Dear Joe: Ms. P has nothing to add to your letter. Are you listening, men of America? Happy Valentine's Day!

The Most Beautiful Words

July. It's that time of year. It hasn't started yet, but I can tell it's just around the corner. Pretty soon, you won't be able to pick up a newspaper or a magazine without some self-appointed town crier informing you that Henry James thought *summer afternoon* were two of the most beautiful words in the English language.

Summer! Afternoon!

I grind my teeth every time I see that quote, and by August I've usually worked up to a full-blown migraine aura. I know Henry James is supposed to be a literary genius and all that, but he needs to leave his weather/linguistic analysis up to somebody who's a little more grounded in reality and triple-digit temperatures. Frankly, I think he spent a bit too much time in London. If he'd ever been to Texas in July, he would have come up with a different, less mellifluous quote and much shorter novels.

To me, the words *summer* and *afternoon*, when welded together, produce a stagnant, polluted stream of conscious-ness—*sunstroke! Teeming ant beds! White-hot streets and sidewalks! Sweat! Spiraling utility bills!* But most of all, *torpor! fatigue! and lethargy!*—and I'd haul out the thesaurus for more synonyms, but the truth is I'm feeling kind of torpid myself today.

Which brings me—torpor, that is—to the teenagers in my house. I'm pretty certain that the epicenter of summer torpor is in our living room. Kids are sprawled everywhere in the living room, propped up by large pieces of furniture, barely able to clutch remote controls in their (formerly small, now newly) large, clammy hands. Two or three times a day, my husband and I give the two who are related to us a pep talk. We speak about what a wonderful institution a summer job is—a fabulous experience, really! Something they'll never forget!

We're big believers in summer jobs, we tell them over and over. They formed our character, molded us, and look how we turned out. We'd be happy to talk about the city dump where their father worked one summer or the hours their mother spent typing. The thrill of earning their own money. The pride of having their own bank account. The coffee breaks, the W-4 forms, the fascinating colleagues. (Funny, the further we are away from it all, the more sentimental we become.)

Our daughter lands a job at a neighborhood store and spends her time memorizing codes for broccoli and radishes and peas. We redouble our efforts with her brother, who appears to be of the Maynard G. Krebbes School of Ambition.

Get a job? His eyes expand into electric blue pools of horror. "I'm only *fourteen*," says the kid who spends much of his life telling us we treat him like a baby, don't give him enough responsibility or allowance, don't realize how old and mature he really and truly is, for Pete's sake. "Aren't there child labor laws?" he wants to know. Tragedy snakes through his voice: He sounds like he's practicing for Hamlet's soliloquy.

The days pass, and he takes occasional, lucrative babysitting jobs that seem to involve talking on the phone, eating pizza, and watching TV. He always returns with his pockets stuffed with bills, his energy kaput. "As long as he's working at something, it's okay," his father says.

I agree with him, mainly because of all this summer-torpor stuff. After all, who am I to talk, going through my own summer of slothfulness? What kind of summer role model am I, anyway?

The heat skyrockets and our house is a mess and the grass needs to be cut. So what have I been up to lately? I always hate it when people ask me that. I try to hint that I'm doing something time-consuming and important—writing a new book, say, or learning Esperanto. But no. I write a few sentences and I'm exhausted. I turn to my new, unhealthy obsession with the book rankings of Amazon.com, a system that's designed to ratchet up the neurosis of already skittish, emotionally fragile writers. That's why I drive to yoga a lot, till the air-conditioning in my car gives out.

"We can't get you in for a couple of weeks," says the woman at the car-repair office. Why? "Oh, you know," she says, "everybody brings their car in to get fixed in the summer."

I make an appointment two weeks from now. "Everybody's going on vacation right now," the woman says soothingly. "It'll be easier in the fall."

Her words linger after I hang up the phone and decide not to drive my car till after dark for the next several days.

Someday it will be fall. It will be easier. It will be cooler. I think I've found a few of my own most beautiful words in the English language.

Just Another First Day of School

Every year my friend Betsy and I get together for lunch to celebrate the first day of school. It's a tradition. We toast ourselves with ice water and coffee and lots of adult conversation. We've made it through another summer!

Oh, sure, I know. Summer signifies freedom to our kids. But not to us. To mothers who have their offices at home, freedom's just another word for the beginning of school.

Our workplaces have cleared out. The noise level is down, the phone's stopped ringing every five seconds, and when it does, it might actually be for one of us. We're back on a schedule. Hard at work. Disciplined once again. Sure, it might still be 600 degrees outside, but the beginning of school always makes me think there's a nip in the air.

This year we are joined by our friends Linda and Leila. Leila has taken her two sons to grade school, Linda has dropped her daughter off at grade school, and Betsy has gotten her two sons off to middle school and grade school. They all talk so much about the first day of school—teachers! backpacks! carpools!—that we even forget to toast each other.

I listen to them for several minutes, following the conversation like a fast ping-pong match. Then I plunge in. Sometimes you have to do that around a bunch of big talkers, or you'll end up brooding into your cappuccino for months.

"Let me tell you about our first day of school," I announce. The three of them stare at me.

It had been different. As usual, we'd forced our resident population of back-to-schoolers onto the front porch so we could take our annual photograph. But for the first time in years, we had only one child, our son, going back to school. He'd knotted his face into a scowl when we cornered him with the camera. Pictures were for little kids, and he was in high school now, in case we hadn't noticed. But he'd posed anyway, since we threatened that he'd have to walk to school otherwise. The camera clicked and whirred as he broke into a grudging half-smile.

One child on the front porch. How do you celebrate the beginning of school when your older child is going off to college and hasn't left yet and you know everything's changing so fast that you can't even see it, but you feel it somewhere in the pit of your stomach, like the steep dive on a plane? It isn't the same, at all. Nothing's the same.

I tell my friends how I'd spied a baby in the grocery store the day before. She had a perfect bald head and soft, downy fuzz close to her neck. She looked exactly as our daughter had

85

looked eighteen years ago. The minute I saw her, I wanted to pick her up and bury my face in her little neck and inhale that wonderful scent of her. All of a sudden, I wanted to throw myself down in the middle of the produce section and sob.

Betsy, Linda, and Leila stare at me, their eyes wide. They don't say much, except that Linda says she's pretty sure I'm going to need a support group for all this, and maybe we should schedule another lunch very soon.

She has a point. "We were depressed for months after our son left for college," another friend, Roberta, had told me a few weeks ago. "We all sat at the table and stared at each other. We couldn't even talk for months."

Depression. Silent dinners. That's what lies before us. Great. In the meantime, I was having small breakdowns close to a tilted pile of unshucked corn. "Are you going to miss your sister?" I ask our son. He shrugs, another one of those cool gestures he's recently picked up. "I can't wait to move into her room," he says. "I'll have my own bathroom."

School's started, but at our house, we're still on hold. Waiting for something to happen. Getting more testy and emotional with each other. Packing and rearranging and talking and trying to remember if we've said everything we need to say. We've forgotten lots of things, haven't we? Neglected to tell her—about what? Didn't we know this time would come, that she'd leave the house for college? Yes, of course, we did. No, of course, we didn't. Not really.

So, after all these years, your first child leaves you. She steps on a plane today, as a matter of fact, at seven in the morning and hurtles thousands of miles away to a new, exciting life.

Another first day of school, but everything's different. We'll be fine, I tell myself. We'll all adjust. Someday, I'll be able to cruise the produce section with abandon, squeezing cantaloupes and chiles and ripe nectarines. I'll hardly even notice that baby over there, because I won't need to. I already know the scent of a baby's soft neck, and it's the sweetest smell on earth.

——————— 🍎 ———————

The Christmas Spirit

We hadn't even finished our Thanksgiving leftovers, and I was already seriously testy about the upcoming holiday season.

It was all too much. Started too early and stayed too long. Cost too much. Served too much food and drink and forced good cheer. The malls swarmed and the Muzak swelled, and I thought I'd probably go bananas if I heard "The Little Drummer Boy" one more time.

At home, my husband was already planning his annual Christmas lights display. "It's going to be Picasso-esque this year," he told me.

That cheered me up, until I recalled that, year after year, our Christmas lights stayed up till spring, and I always had to scream and throw things to get him to take them down. One year our lights were still up in May, and my husband had told me he had the "complete support" of all the men in the neighborhood to leave them up for the rest of the year. In our neighborhood, I figured, all you had to do was pass out a few free beers and all the men would be in "complete support" of invading Oklahoma with their bottle rockets and minivans.

So I was thoroughly grumpy by the time I sat down to read the newspaper and discovered the story of the "airborn" baby. "Listen to this," I told my husband and daughter.

The day before Thanksgiving, Theresa de Bara, thirty-five, had gone into labor on a TWA flight from New York to Orlando.

Her contractions grew more severe, and another passenger—an internist who mistakenly thought he was on vacation—was drafted to deliver the baby. As the plane began an emergency descent into Dulles International Airport in Washington, D.C., the baby was born with his umbilical cord wrapped around his neck. He turned blue and wasn't breathing.

Two other passengers, who were paramedics, suctioned the baby's lungs with a straw from a juice box. They helped the doctor give the baby CPR until he began to breathe. Connie Duquette, a flight attendant, requisitioned another passenger's shoelaces to tie the baby's umbilical cord. Then she got on the plane's public-address system to announce, "It's a boy."

"The cabin erupted in cheers and applause," I read aloud. "The flight attendants were crying. So was the baby."

So was I by this time. I finished reading about how the baby's health looked promising, and how the passengers gave the doctor and mother an "emotional standing ovation." My husband got up to wipe his eyes, and our daughter looked at us as if we were dimwitted.

"What are you crying about?" she asked.

Well, nothing, I thought. And everything.

I was thinking, too, about the time two or three years ago, when I'd been part of a much smaller group than the one I'd read about. We were in a shopping center, instead of a plane, and we gathered to try to help a man who was having a heart attack in his car. Like the baby, he almost died, but then he was saved by a doctor and nurse who were passing by.

The few of us who stood there, trying to help, didn't know each other. We didn't know the man who'd had the heart attack. We'd been caught, by accident, but once we were there, we couldn't leave. We stayed till the ambulance took him away and we heard he'd survived the heart attack.

Since then, I've never been to that shopping center once without thinking about that man I didn't know and the strangers I stood with, clutching each other's arms and hoping out loud. I can't remember what season it was when all of this happened. But like the "airborn" baby, it was the kind of Christmas story I needed. You know, the kind of story where you look into strangers' eyes and hearts and realize you're not alone after all.

———— 🍎 ————

Holiday Newsletters, Round 1

I know, I know. Xeroxed letters at Christmas are impersonal and irritating, and everyone hates them.

But after all my ungrateful friends started complaining about my chatty, handwritten letters because they couldn't read my writing, I knew it was time to bail out. Why torture myself? I started mass-mailing typed letters.

What I've learned over the past two years is that when it comes to photocopied holiday letters, it really is better to give than to receive. But writing these letters doesn't have to be unbearable. Just follow a few simple guidelines:

- *Set the tone immediately in your first paragraph.* Make it breezy and cheerful. Tell everyone again and again how busy you are—what with work and family and social obligations.

  This is critical. No one wants to hear from someone who isn't busy, and they may not even finish your letter if it's clear you have lots of time on your hands. (And besides, if you're not that busy, why aren't you slaving over chatty, handwritten notes?)

- *Devote a paragraph to every member of your immediate family who lives at home, whether you want them there or not.* This includes children over the age of thirty who've returned to the nest and don't leave their rooms for days at a time and start to hyperventilate when you inquire about their job prospects.

Save your own news for the last, and don't refer to yourself in the third person, unless you've been diagnosed with multiple personalities or you're running for political office.

- ◆ *If you have really great news, bury it.* No one likes an obvious brag sheet, and you don't want to ruin all your friends' Christmases, do you?

So it's best only to hint at wonderful news. Or to attach it to something that's self-deprecating. This shows that success hasn't spoiled you.

BAD EXAMPLE: "Guess what! Nigel won the Nobel Prize for the second time!!! We don't know what we're going to do with all the money!"

(Oh, gross. Unless Nigel uses his money to check himself into the Betty Ford Clinic, no one wants to hear this. And the second time? Come on. Who counts Nobels, anyway? Also, get a grip on all those exclamation marks. You're not supposed to hyperventilate in Christmas letters.)

BETTER EXAMPLE: "Stockholm was miserably cold this year. Fortunately, Nigel didn't have to give his acceptance speech in Swedish. He's still hopeless at languages!"

(There! Much better. You've only hinted at Nigel's honor, and you've made it clear he remains an endearing idiot in lots of ways. Best yet, you may have some friends left to write to next Christmas.)

- ◆ *If you have bad news, bury that too.* It's the holiday season, and people don't want to hear lots of downers.

BAD EXAMPLE: "You've probably heard that Fred left me and moved in with some sleazy little tramp. I've hired the greediest, most unethical divorce lawyer in town, and he says we can sue the pants off Fred, assuming he ever keeps them on these days."

(Quel bummer! Who wants to read something this disheartening?)

BETTER EXAMPLE: "I'm sure you'll all join me in wishing Fred and his new child bride the best! This is a fabulous opportunity for her, after all those years of in-breeding in her family."

(Perfect. In a very gentle way, this lets people know you and Fred have taken different paths. It also helps to introduce Fred's new wife to all your friends and to show you certainly harbor no grudges.)

  ◆ *Like Christmas presents, these letters need to be wrapped up quickly.* Make the ending snappy and upbeat, and mention again how busy you are.

P.S. If you've had a really bad year, forget about typing and mass mailing, and write a chatty, handwritten note. If your handwriting is as bad as mine, no one will be able to read it, anyway.

———— 🍎 ————

Holiday Newsletters, Round 2

BULLETIN TO ALL AMERICANS:

You may not realize it, but the laws have recently changed. Due to last year's outbreak of mass psychosis that resulted from other people's photocopied holiday letters, we in the Post Office's National Self-Esteem Department have decided to move proactively.

This year, before you can send out your family's annual newsletter, you're required to pass the following Holiday Newsletter Qualifying Test. So back away from that printer now! Tear your hands off that copy machine! This is the government talking. Be as honest as you are about your tax returns!

1) If you could describe your family's past year in a single word, what would that word be?

   a) Better. At least no one got arrested this year.

   b) Fabulous, comme toujours! Of course, Nigel's winning his second Nobel was a complete shock to us!

   c) Pernicious.

2) Are you prepared for the holidays?

   a) Just about. We've almost paid off our bills from Christmas 1994.

   b) What a silly question. Naturally, I'm prepared. I finished my shopping in June, and I've been baking since Labor Day. I can't bear to disappoint all my many friends who expect me to deliver their usual dozen hand-decorated Sacher tortes for the season!

   c) No. My doctor refused to renew my prescription for extra-strength tranquilizers, which is my usual present to myself this time of year. So I fired the quack.

3) Describe the perfect holiday dinner.

   a) Oh, wow. No screaming, no fighting, no divorces before dessert, no salmonella poisoning, and no severe food allergies that require hospitalization. (Also, no accidental arson with the candles on the table being used to set your sister's hair on fire. That wasn't funny, Jason!)

b) Vivaldi on the stereo. A flawless table set with my heirloom china, incredibly valuable candelabra, and artistically arranged fresh flowers in vintage goldfish bowls. Braised pheasant with seared artichoke hearts. Risotto a la Milanese. Homemade pastries and hors d'oeuvres. Riveting intellectual conversation in several of the Romance languages.

c) A dinner somebody else cooks. My sister-in-law, for example. She hasn't had our family over for fourteen years. (*Are you reading this, Marcia?* Isn't it about time you got off your big, fat derriere and baked a 25-pound turkey till you burn it, as usual? What are you waiting for—the Second Coming?)

4) Any news you'd like to share about your husband?

a) No, fortunately! After all those big headlines about his embezzling money from his bankrupt company, he's keeping a very low profile.

b) Well, I've already mentioned Nigel's second Nobel. But I believe I failed to mention his latest MacArthur Genius Award. Isn't that adorable?

c) Who's this (b) person? She's getting on my nerves.

5) Tell us about your children.

a) Well, Jason's been busy, busy, busy ever since he joined that gang. And Ashley's hair has finally grown back after last Christmas' inferno, and she has several new, interesting pierced places all over her body.

b) Oh, dear, I hate to brag. But Fiona just graduated summa from Dartmouth, where she was elected Ice Queen four years in a row! And Trevor has just been named a National Merit Scholar. I'm surprised he has time to maintain his 4.0 average with such an active social life!

   c) Is it just me? Or is there a stomach virus going around?

6) Do you have any cute pet stories?

   a) Well, our cat, Blanche DuBois, threw herself out of a tree, and she's now under suicide watch at the vet's. Is that a cute story?

   b) Oh, do I ever! Our bichon frise, Miss Lou-Lou, absolutely knocked them dead at the Tri-County Canine Round-Up and received the Best of Show Award. But she doesn't think she's a dog! Oh, no! She thinks she's a person!

   c) Oh, yeah? Miss Lou-Lou and (b) must have a lot in common.

7) What about any great new diets you can recommend for the new year?

   a) I'm starting a designer water diet on New Year's Day to get rid of the 75 pounds I've gained this year. It's supposed to take three weeks. Do you think that's realistic?

   b) Oh, dear! My metabolism is so high that I've never been bigger than a size 4. But I do recommend working out with a highly skilled personal trainer, like Biff LaBonte. It's so fabulous to have a sensitive, caring confidant like Biff. It's given new meaning to my already exquisite life.

   c) Can't somebody shut her up? Won't somebody refill my prescription? If there's really a Santa Claus, I know what I'll find in my stocking! Xanax. Loads of Xanax. I'll be good next year, I promise!

All right, quit your whining. Let's make this snappy. Score your answers.

Mostly a)'s and c)'s: You've passed! You can write all the holiday letters you want. The post office salutes you! Hearing about your lives should cheer up the rest of the country!

Mostly b)'s: We're very sorry, but you're ineligible to send out a holiday newsletter this year. No exceptions will be made. Please—think of this year's silence as your gift to the rest of the world.

———— 🍎 ————

Holiday Newsletters, Round 3

SECOND ANNUAL BULLETIN TO ALL AMERICANS

FROM: THE U.S. POSTAL SERVICE'S NATIONAL SELF-ESTEEM DEPARTMENT

You didn't listen, did you?

Last year you had to pass a test before we'd let you send out your usual mass mailing of good cheer and cheesy self-aggrandizement. Did you take the test? No, you didn't. You kept pumping out the letters and slapping stamps on them, and we had to deal with the usual holiday epidemic of paranoid bitterness resulting from hearing about how great everybody else's lives are.

This year, in the spirit of giving, we've designed a list of holiday rules to follow while composing your family's newsletter. If you don't follow these rules, your newsletters will be fed into a paper shredder and used to stuff highly uncomfortable mattresses you may have to sleep on someday:

1) Stop bragging about your kids. Many important psychological studies have shown that children whose parents yak about them too much in their annual newsletters suffer from tragically low self-esteem, a startlingly high rate of acne, bad posture, twitching, and hats worn backward; worst of all, *they have no chance whatsoever of getting into an Ivy League school.*

   Do you want to ruin your child's chances of getting into Harvard before he's toilet-trained? We don't think so. Brag about the weather or your okra crop, instead.

2) God may be in the details, but good holiday newsletters aren't. When in doubt, cut to the chase. Or just cut, period.

   BAD EXAMPLE: Our teenage daughter, Ashley, is now exploring her expanding personhood through multiple nostril and lip piercings and her newly shaved and tattooed head. You wouldn't believe how pesky those nostril rings are when you have a bad cold!

   GOOD EXAMPLE: We're the parents of a teenager. You fill in the blanks.

3) If you say something funny, don't follow it with *ha, ha!* When you add a verbal laugh track so your audience will chuckle at something hilarious, either a) it really isn't that hilarious in the first place or b) your audience completely lacks a sense of humor (in which case, you should be asking yourself, *Why am I writing these people, anyway?*)

4) Avoid intrusively emotional or physical extremes when speaking about your spouse or partner.

   BAD EXAMPLE: Nigel and I are still ravenously passionate lovebirds, just as we were when we met each other over 35 years ago! Our sex life is hotter than ever! Who needs Viagra?

(Oh, gross. Who needs his stomach pumped? Your whole mailing list, that's who.)

EQUALLY BAD EXAMPLE: I should have listened to my mother about Nigel. She warned me that he'd be fat, bald, and bankrupt someday. Well, Mama forgot something. He's a drunken lout, too!

(How interesting. Did old Mama also suggest Nigel would be marrying the Wicked Witch of the West?)

BETTER EXAMPLE: Nigel and I continue, as always.

(Perfect! This sentence is subtle and mysterious—qualities that are sorely lacking in most holiday newsletters. No one will have the faintest idea what you mean.)

5) Sentences about animals that "think they're people!" are hereby subject to fines of $10,000 per utterance. Sentences about people who "think they're animals!" may continue, however.

6) Don't confuse what you tell your friends with what you tell your family physician.

BAD EXAMPLE: Then, after I'd vomited for three days straight, they had to put a tube down my stomach, which was similar to swallowing a garden hose. On top of that, my recent onslaught of post-pregnancy incontinence is getting worse, and I'm afraid that adult diapers are just around the corner.

GOOD EXAMPLE: I had the stomach flu this year. Didn't everybody?

7) It's really nice—*so* nice!—that you trekked all over Bali, the Arctic Circle, and Casablanca this year, and we're sure everyone is just devastated to have missed

your slides. But keep a low travelogue profile, unless you were a) deported in the trunk of a compact car with six complete strangers or b) thrown in jail and tortured with high-volume renditions of Gary Puckett and the Union Gap.

8) Please limit yourself to a maximum of three exclamation marks per letter. Otherwise, you give the impression you're panting, which is an unattractive response to the holiday season and may lead to concerns you've fallen off your twelve-step program.

9) Finally, before you send out your newsletter, read it carefully and ask yourself, "Would I enjoy receiving this letter?" If so, why bother sending it to anyone? *You may be your own best audience.* Just think of all the postage you'll save!

Chapter 6

Cultural Trends

Stunt Doubles—Why Not?

All right. I admit it. I stole the original idea from my friend Martha. She deserves all the credit.

You see, this time last year, Martha was about to have surgery. She was in the operating room, and a small armada of doctors, nurses, and technicians were gathered around her. It was time for the general anesthesia, and the situation was serious. Naturally, everyone looked very sober, apprehensive, and grim.

"Wait a minute," Martha said loudly.

All the medical personnel stopped what they were doing and stared at her. They were all quiet.

"Isn't it time for my stunt double to come in?" Martha asked.

The whole room stared at her, shocked. Finally, they realized she was joking. (Well, kind of.) Then they laughed.

Every time I think about that story, I smile. *A stunt double! Why didn't I think of that?*

I always love it when the atmosphere is serious, pompous, and life threatening, and somebody like Martha manages to crack a joke. I think she also deserves lots of bonus points because 1) it was her life that was being threatened; and 2) she made her doctors laugh—and doctors are what I would call a serious breed and a hard audience, especially when they're hauling scalpels around.

But most of all, I love that story because it's so inspiring. In half the situations in my life, I now wonder: *Hey, wait a minute! Where's my stunt double?*

My dentist says I need a new crown and more gum surgery. I drive a car pool, and someone throws up in my back seat. The toilet backs up. The cat lays a half-dead pigeon at my feet in the living room. I'm actually expected to climb up on that Stairmaster and pump and sweat for a half-hour. It's time to do our income tax.

Where's my stunt double, anyway? I keep waiting for her, but she stands me up again and again. Maybe she needs directions to get to my dentist's office.

I'm pretty sure I have lots of more important and creative things to do with my life, such as eating bon-bons, talking on the phone, and reading Proust without going into a coma. Sure, I might do windows, but I really don't like overflowing toilets. That must be somebody else's job. Didn't I put that in my contract? I don't do anything messy, unhygienic, painful, or dangerous.

I am ready to delegate. I am eager to delegate. I am great at delegating. But how can I delegate when there's no one around but me?

I talk to my friend Pamela about it, and I quickly realize the situation is even worse than I thought. Pamela is an artist, and she thinks that—aside from going to the dentist—most artists and writers also need stunt doubles to make public appearances for them.

"It's not good to look bourgeois or balanced if you're an artist," she says. "Artists are supposed to be strange. I can do the art, but I need someone who's younger and hipper than I am to come to my shows. Mentally deranged would be nice, too."

Pamela has a point, I think. She's right.

"No one used to care what you looked like, how you talked, or what a rotten personality you had if you were a writer," I tell her. "Now, you're supposed to be pithy, profound, and witty and look great on a book jacket. Good cheekbones are quite important."

The longer Pamela and I talk, the more I realize *we're not talking about stunt doubles any longer. We're talking about stunt upgrades*. This is a serious business. You have to be careful when you're picking out a stunt upgrade for public appearances. We're talking about our careers here. We're talking about our images.

Pamela decides her stunt upgrade should probably be wild-eyed, incoherent, and deeply disturbed, with lots of body hair. That would show how creative and profound her art is. I decide my stunt upgrade would be drop-dead gorgeous, scintillating, and devastatingly clever. She'd wear Calvin Klein all the time, and somebody else would pick up the tab. That would get me—I mean *us*—on the *Today* show.

That's all I need in my life, that's all I want for Christmas this year. First, my stunt double will handle my crises, my dirty bathrooms, my dental appointments, and my physical exercise. Maybe she'll even finish that novel I go around claiming I'm writing right now.

My stunt upgrade will show up to take the credit, and she'll flash those cheekbones that could cut a pound of hard cheddar. Oh, Mr. DeMille! Sigourney Weaver is ready for my close-ups now.

Tales of the Telecommuter

Telecommuting is the wave of the future. I know that because I've read it everywhere. (All right, all right. So I've just read it twice, and I've forgotten where it was, exactly. The point is, I know a trend when I see it more than once.)

No more clogged freeways teeming with overheated cars and enraged drivers! No more office wardrobe expenses! No more wasted time hanging around the water cooler, listening to boring old office gossip about who's getting—well, never mind. No more long, tedious meetings where the boss drones on and on about being a team player, multitasking, and brainstorming!

You are going to be a telecommuter! You're on the cutting edge! Get ready to love your life even more!

And so on.

Listen, I really hate to rain on anybody's tirade. But I'm pretty sure that all these prognosticators are nuts. They have stars in their eyes and large, vacant spaces where their brains should be. They're people who have never telecommuted in their lives, since they're too busy brainstorming, multitasking, and hanging around the water cooler at work. But they think telecommuting is a great idea for everybody else.

Well, I'm one of those everybody else people. I've telecommuted, more or less, for years—writing, e-mailing, and faxing from my home office—and I think these soothsayers should get a few clues from people like me. Working from home isn't as easy or as purely wonderful as they like to think.

Here's what I've learned after several years:

1) Some days, you will miss your old job, no matter how terrible it was. That's because you can get a tiny bit *strange* staying at home and being by yourself all the

time. Remember Jack Nicholson in *The Shining*? He was a telecommuter, sort of.

If you find yourself looking forward to telemarketers' calls, desperate to hear your name mangled and mispronounced, you aren't becoming a kinder and gentler person. You are becoming deranged. (Which may also explain why you've recently begun to have long, intimate conversations with your cats, asking their advice about your love life.) Try to get out for lunch more frequently.

2) You won't miss those long, drawn-out meetings at work, but you *will* miss the office gossip like crazy. So what if the stories weren't true? At least they were interesting. And let's face it. You and the cats don't do anything that's nearly that interesting.

3) Step outside your office door, and you'll find your kitchen. Yes, you're right. It's still a mess.

4) Sure, you won't have to invest in a snappy office wardrobe, and it really doesn't matter how you look, since you're by yourself all the time. But there will be days when you'll get totally demoralized just looking at yourself. *Uncombed hair, tattered T-shirt, ragged cutoffs, and sandals? This is you?*

Not everybody feels this way, of course. I have friends who even work in their pajamas, and they tell me it's wonderful. But I couldn't do it. I could be sitting at the computer, channeling the genius of Herman Melville and writing a sequel to *Moby Dick* or something—and if I looked down and saw myself working in pajamas, I would die. I'm sure great works of art have been created in nightclothes, but it's never going to happen to me. If it's 9 A.M. and I'm still not dressed, I'm a failure.

5) By the way, if you step outside your office again, the laundry room is pretty close, too. And no, those clothes haven't folded themselves.

6) When you work at home, no one ever thinks you're really working. That explains why they don't mind calling you to talk for hours about their personal problems or asking you to do a favor, since you're already at home and have lots of free time on your hands.

7) Whenever there's a school holiday (and these times occur constantly, to my mind), you'll find you are much less lonely. That's fine for about five action-filled moments or so. After that, the constant battering of your office door, the garbled screams and wrestling matches over the remote control, and the shrieked insults may interfere with your concentration.

   If you find you've developed the ability to work through a maelstrom like this, it isn't necessarily good news. Your zen-like state may be a symptom of dementia. Consult your yoga teacher or therapist, as applicable.

8) Finally, at some point, something truly dramatic will happen. You'll be offered a regular job. You can return to the office, look nice every day, and have regular office hours and normal office friendships, and you'll never be lonely again! You can stop all this telecommuting stuff and end all this isolation you've been complaining about!

You turn the offer down, of course. What do they think you are—a moron?

Forget it. You're a telecommuter! The wave of the future! Besides, how could you possibly give up all this freedom?

First Names and Formalities

I did it again. I embarrassed my whole family so badly that they just wanted to die.

We were at our next-door neighbors' house, eating guacamole, downing soft drinks, and grousing about how everybody on earth had made a killing in the stock market except us. For some reason, the question came up about how our children should address our neighbors and how their children should address my husband and me. (Our two children are adolescents who like to consider themselves junior adults, except when it comes to picking up the tab in restaurants or loading the dishwasher; our neighbors' two children are much younger.)

"First names are fine with us," our neighbor said. "In fact, we prefer it." Her husband nodded in agreement.

"So do I," my husband said.

Everyone looked at me expectantly.

"I know it sounds old-fashioned," I said apologetically, "but I really would prefer all the children use titles and last names."

They all looked at me like I'd fallen face-first into the soup tureen. There was a long, embarrassed silence, and then everyone started to talk. *Oh, that's fine! Why, sure! No problem!*

"I just wanted to die when you said that," our daughter announced after we got home. "It was awful. I was humiliated."

"We're living in Austin now," my husband pointed out, like I'd forgotten our address or something. "Austin's extremely informal. Everyone in Austin's on a first-name basis."

So what? I thought sulkily. Big deal. Everyone in Austin also has a tip jar by the cash register so you'll feel like a cheapskate if you don't leave a bunch of money in it. Does that mean

I should get a tip jar next to my computer? (So far, this widespread trend hasn't passed on to doctors' or lawyers' offices, but I'm sure it's only a matter of time. Great. I'm already a nervous wreck about offending the college kids who foam my lattes, so I can hardly wait for the day my oncologist gets a tip jar.)

The point is, I like Austin a lot—but I don't have to go native on everything, do I?

Besides, it's a matter of principle. I don't want to be on an automatic first-name basis with everybody—especially with young children. (In fact, I used to say I didn't want to be on a first-name basis with anyone who's still in diapers. But the older my friends and I get, lurching toward a future that probably includes adult diapers, I realize I had better start searching for a new demarcation.)

More than anything, I'm sick and tired of all this chumminess and instant intimacy. As long as I'm looking for someone to blame, it might as well be TV talk shows that broadcast formerly private behavior and conversations into millions of households. If you're on *The Jerry Springer Show*, say, talking about how your nocturnal tastes run to barnyard animals, then doubtless you won't object to everyone using your first name—or that of your animal companion.

It's a little too late for that kind of formality. Besides, the audience is already chanting *Jer-rrry, Jerr-rry, Jer-rry*, not *Mr. Springer, Mr. Springer, Mr. Springer.*

I know, I know. It's a losing battle that I keep howling about. In person, I'm actually a very friendly, informal sort. Just try to give me five or ten minutes before we become best friends and confidantes, since I have this irrational, antiquated *thing* about instant intimacy. Is that too much to ask?

I suppose so. That's what I thought while my husband and I sat and listened to a saleswoman who set up our cell phone account last month. She told us how we could phone from anywhere. She told us that we could stay on the phone for 300 minutes or something like that. She told us that the audio quality was so great that we wouldn't hear static.

She talked and talked for at least 300 minutes, I'm pretty sure, and at the end of every sentence, she used my first name repeatedly, kind of like it was a nouveau punctuation mark. So I sat there and wondered what to say.

"I'm sorry, we haven't been properly introduced." (No! Too defensive and old-fashioned!)

"Put a lid on it, sister." (Uh-uh. Shows I've been watching *The Godfather* a little too often.)

"Actually, I don't go by my first name. My best friends call me the duchess of Windsor."

And so on. I didn't do any of those things, naturally. I just sat and listened while my first name sprouted up again and again, like popcorn in a microwave. The trouble is, even more than disliking this kind of intrusive intimacy, I hate hurting people's feelings when they're basically well meaning.

You can see my problem, I'm sure. With a first name like mine, that kind of ruthlessness comes hard.

Pardon Me If I Sit

A few weeks ago, my husband and I went to a traveling version of a big Broadway musical. I'm not an expert on musicals or anything, but even I noticed it was a lackluster performance. So what? They got a standing ovation.

Later some friends and I went to see a one-woman play that was very good. She got a standing ovation, too.

And let's not forget the famous comedienne who came to town. She got a standing ovation before she began her routine. After she finished, she got another one.

Then there was our son's middle-school band. It played capably, and the members were cute, all dressed up. You can guess the rest.

"What doesn't get a standing ovation these days?" sniffs my friend Alice.

I have no idea. Woody Allen said 80 percent of success is showing up, but he never mentioned that you get a standing ovation for it.

Play after play, performance after performance, I sit in the audience and feel like a curmudgeon because I'm not jumping to my feet like everybody else around me. But I don't want to give in to the social pressure, and the truth is, I'm embarrassed to be part of an audience that's so easy and grateful that everything's deemed spectacular. Enough. Not everybody deserves to be rewarded.

My next-door neighbor Leila has already indicated I'm extremely boring on the whole subject of standing ovations. "Who's offended you now?" she wants to know. I tell her about the middle-school band concert, and she looks shocked that any mother could be so stingy with her praise.

"I bet they worked really hard," she says.

"I know they worked really hard," I say. "But that doesn't mean they should get a standing ovation for it. What are they going to expect when they really do something wonderful? Cartwheels? Cadillacs?"

Leila nods placatingly. I can tell she thinks I'm a little deranged. But that isn't how I see myself—at least most of the time. I'm worried that all this standing-ovation inflation doesn't have anybody like Alan Greenspan to monitor it. After being lavished so liberally and indiscriminately, it becomes meaningless. Where do you go from there? What's the matter with just a lot of vigorous applause for something that's good but not great?

But no. They hand out standing ovations routinely these days, the way they hand out trophies. If your child's soccer team places fifth in the neighborhood league, they'll give out trophies the size of a soccer field. Just imagine what the kids will expect if they ever place fourth. You'll have to move to a bigger house.

"Can we get a limousine for my birthday?" our newly teenage son wants to know. One of his friends just got a limousine to take him and his buddies to some kind of video palace for his birthday. To hear our son talk, it was one of life's peak experiences. But now it's over. Your first ride in a limousine when you're this young. What a waste.

"Can we?" he asks again.

Fat chance, his father and I say. He hints that it's clear his friend's mother loves her son more than his cheapskate parents love him. We don't take the bait.

It's all the same to me, really, all this reward inflation and the jadedness that inevitably follows. I want to save things, to savor them—cars, trophies, standing ovations—and to enjoy them more because they're longer in coming.

I want—well, I'll tell you what I want it to be like. Six years ago our daughter was in the middle school orchestra. At a concert that year, one of her friends stood in front of the orchestra to play a solo on her violin. Her name was Sun Joo, and she was from Korea. She stood there awkwardly, a thin, serious girl, facing an audience of parents and families. I'd guess that most of us were afraid she couldn't do it.

But she did. The minute she raised her violin, she gathered force and exhilaration. She played beautifully—music that mesmerized all of us. She played flawlessly for 10 or 15 minutes, and I can't even tell you the name of the piece she performed. But all the time she played, no one moved. We were all riveted.

Then she finished and stood there with her violin, an uncertain child again. We all leapt to our feet, shouting and applauding as hard as we could. It was thrilling to have witnessed something so unusual and brilliant, and I still get chills when I think about it.

That's what I want. It's all I'm asking for. If it isn't that wonderful, that memorable, then forget it. I'm not going to stand for it.

———————— 🍎 ————————

The Optimism Police

All right, all right. I admit it. I was already feeling a little crabby when a friend from a state I won't name forwarded an e-mail message last week. But I was dying for anything to distract me from the writing I wasn't doing, so I read the whole thing.

It was the story of a guy named Jerry. Jerry was a great guy. He was a hard worker and a good family man. No matter what happened to him, he responded optimistically. He saw the cup as half-full. His glasses were rose-colored. You get the picture.

I hadn't read very far, but Jerry was already starting to get on my nerves. I kept on reading, though. I was ready for some kind of dark O. Henry twist to the story.

That's when I got to the point about how Jerry's restaurant was held up and the robbers shot him several times. By the time he got to the hospital, Jerry was lying on a stretcher, almost dead. A nurse asked aloud what Jerry was allergic to, and Jerry raised his head. "I'm allergic to bullets!" he said. The whole emergency room burst into laughter, and Jerry then told them to save his life. Which they did.

You always have a choice, the e-mail pointed out. You can react positively to life's events, like old Jerry, or you can react negatively. You could send the e-mail message on to other friends and help them have a great day, or you could delete it. It was your choice. It was up to you.

By this time I was brooding so hard I almost had a nose-bleed. So much for dark O. Henry twists. This was another one of those cloying feel-good-or-we'll-bludgeon-you messages from the group I like to call the Optimism Police. (The OP are different from ordinary optimists, a group I happen to like and wouldn't dream of criticizing unless I was in a really foul mood. Some of my best friends are optimists. I'm even married to one. Ordinary optimists are relaxed and tolerant, and they have a sense of humor. The OP are rigid and self-righteous. They're the kind of people who carefully memorize a joke and then introduce it by saying, "This is a very funny story," which it almost never is.)

These days you can see members of the Optimism Police almost everywhere you go (although I've noticed they frequently hang around the frozen-food counters at local grocery stores, halfway between the broccoli and lima beans). They walk in a lock step of forced good cheer and iron-on smiles. Their eyes blaze and their teeth are gritted, and their hearts are fervent, messianic, and smug. Every day they run the gamut of emotions from A to A-plus. When you happen on them, it's like being attacked by a flock of tone-deaf parakeets chirping the same bad song.

If you aren't one of the OP—if your smile has faltered and your arches have fallen and your outlook is bleak—then no wonder your life is such a mess. You had a choice, and you picked the wrong door, you pessimistic twit. You jumped without a parachute. You have no one to blame but old numero uno.

What especially irks me is that there is a kernel of truth in their thinking. In fact, there's just enough truth to make it confusing. I do happen to believe it's better to go through life with a positive attitude. I do think your attitude is part of the story.

But that isn't enough for the OP. *Your attitude is everything*—that's what a friend of mine who's sick is being told constantly. *Your attitude is the only thing that counts*. But it isn't. Our attitude is something, not everything. Every dark or shadowy emotion we feel isn't a failure of optimistic will. Those emotions are what make us human and fully alive, instead of wind-up toys with the emotional repertoire of a petri dish.

Sure, attitudes can help us, but they don't control everything. Not everything is under our control and not everything is our fault. Life is more complicated than that. In fact, it's often seriously unpredictable, unfair, and out of control. Which is exactly why simple equations like *Your attitude is everything* are so attractive—but so inadequate and often so hurtful and destructive.

Anyway, that's why I deleted the e-mail about Jerry. It was either that or write a whole new ending that showed life's snarls, inequities, and melodramas. I mean, who has the time for stories that long?

———— ☿ ————

Letters for Sale

Privacy, schmivacy. What do I care? If Joyce Maynard can sell her collection of letters from J.D. Salinger at Sotheby's, why can't I sell all my correspondence? (I won't sell my letters from J.D., of course; they're far too personal, and we're both very private people. But everything else. Sure.)

I won't reveal all the details right now—I mean, don't be silly. I'll give you just a glimmer of the caliber of letters I've gotten over the years, and you be the judge. Send your bid to Sotheby's as soon as possible, and make it big as long as you're at it. Joyce Maynard isn't the only one who has kids who are going to college.

Exclusive excerpts from Ruth Pennebaker's letter collection:

Dear Pennebaker Family: Congratulations! The four of you just set a Blockbuster record for never turning in a video on time! Week after week, year after year, you've checked out all kinds of movies and never once returned them in a timely manner! You pay more in penalties than you do in rentals.

What would we be without people like you? Our corporate profits would be nil. Keep up the good work!—Your Friends at Blockbuster Video

Dear Ruth: Thank you so much for having us to your recent dinner party. We thoroughly enjoyed the lively conversation, especially when you and one of your guests got into a screaming brawl over Woody Allen and Soon-Yi Previn. Who would have thought that a tiny little butter knife could have resulted in an emergency-room visit like that? (Hope your homeowner's insurance is up to date!)

As usual, the food was—what's the right word?—memorable. We've never tasted anything quite like the Shrimp Barka dish you and your husband prepared. We remembered it for days afterward. Next time, we'll do the cooking—and you provide the entertainment. Fondly, Rob and Laurie

Dear Ms. Pennebaker: You are a moron. Your last column on soccer moms was the most superficial thing I've ever read in my life. No wonder Rush Limbaugh makes fun of people like you. Next time, try a column with some depth.—A Non-Fan

Dear Parents: If you've noticed your child scratching his or her head recently, it may be due to a recent, unfortunate outbreak of lice at our school. We suspect that outside elements—certainly none of our children or teachers—are responsible for this deplorable incident. Please read the attached brochure about measures required to rid your household of these creatures. Get ready to devote your entire weekend to extensive shampooing, combing, squashing, vacuuming, spraying and washing. Sincerely, Your School Principal

Dear Ms. Pennebaker: We at Weltschmerz Insurance are in receipt of your recent, heartfelt letter begging us to reinstate your homeowner's insurance coverage after two disastrous events at your house. Yes, we agree it was simply bad luck that within the same week, a dinner guest was injured by a butter knife stuck in his left hand, and a hackberry tree fell on your garage, where you and your husband were evidently having an argument at the time. Yes, very bad luck.

Frankly, we at Weltschmerz Insurance prefer not to continue to insure someone who has such bad luck. What do you think we are—a charity? May we suggest psychiatric help? We won't pay for it, but your medical insurance might. Sincerely, Claims Division

Dear Ms. Pennebaker: We haven't heard from you in ages! Please call to make an appointment concerning your gingivitis report, your daughter's latest cavities, and the braces we need to put on your son. By the way, we still haven't seen your husband. Guess you must not have been joking about his dental phobia! Sincerely, Happy Smiles Dental Clinic

Dear Ms. Pennebaker: Our records indicate you may be married. But, as you know, in this chaotic world of ours, nothing is permanent. In case your status has changed, let us know. Our new business, You've Got Male, has been a source of delight and eternal happiness to many, many of our clients. Give us a call!—YGM, Inc.

Dear Parents: Due to the hard work and dedication of our students, parents, and teachers, the recent lice epidemic at our school has been vanquished! That's the good news.

The bad news is that our school is now suffering from a widespread outbreak of pink eye. If your child's eyes are red and crusty, and he or she can't open them, he or she may be suffering from the disease. Please consult your family physician as soon as possible.—Your School Administration

P.S. Although children recover very quickly from pink eye, parents have been known to require two or three weeks to get over it. May we suggest a pair of sunglasses so you don't shock others?

Martha Stewart and Me

I've come to a turning point. I realize that I should stop blaming Martha Stewart for my low self-esteem. My domestic problems are all pre-Martha.

Here I'd resented Martha all these years, just because she did things I could never do. Such as entertain elegantly, stencil the hardwood floors at her beautiful Connecticut farmhouse, bake her own damned bread, keep her hair streaked perfectly, and make millions of dollars from her books, magazines, videos, and TV shows.

That's why I tuned into *Oprah* recently—because I wanted to feel inferior. Martha was going to be on the show, along with members of the Martha fan club and other women like me who didn't like Martha because they thought she was too much of a perfectionist and kind of a showoff.

It was all very interesting. The president of the Martha fan club showed how she lived the "Martha lifestyle," which seems to involve having lots of baskets around. She also uses Martha bed sheets, grows her own herbs, and hangs Martha's picture along with photographs of her children and grandchildren because she considers Martha part of her family.

"I want to be like Martha—but it hasn't affected my individuality," she said.

Some of the other women told Martha they found her a little irritating because she spends her time painting egg-shaped cookies for Easter and landscaping gingerbread replicas of her farmhouse for Christmas and gardening and stenciling and generally looking great. All of which went over like a load of week-old guacamole with these women, since they spent most of their days cleaning up major milk spills in the kitchen and tripping over vacuum cleaners no one ever used and leaving their dirty laundry all over the couch.

The president of the Martha club told them they were way out of line. "Why shouldn't you try to be perfect?" she said. And Martha pointed out that even she, Martha, wasn't perfect anyway, because she skied badly and wasn't good at shopping for herself and she had lots of other faults, too. Then Oprah told Martha that she always looked wonderful, and Martha tried to make Oprah feel better by saying that she'd just gotten her outfit "off the rack."

My twelve-year-old daughter and I were avidly watching all of this, lying on an unmade bed. "Is Martha for real?" my daughter asked.

"As real as we are," I said.

All of which made me think. Here was Martha, selling the glamorously homespun, creative life she lived, and now that I thought about it, that was just fine. Martha was selling what she had to sell.

So why couldn't I do the same? I was practically the same age as Martha, and I've given parties and learned a few things. I had a lifestyle, too! I could market what I know! I could offer my own:

Entertainment Do's and Don'ts

Do act reluctant at first when people ask if they can bring something to a party. Then let them. There will be so much food at the party that no one will realize you haven't contributed anything at all. (Also, after the party's over, you may end up with lots of new serving dishes people forget to take home.)

Do take dips out of the plastic containers and put them in your own dishes. Squish them so they don't keep the shape of the container. This shows class. (No one will believe they're homemade, but you'll get points for presentation.)

Do refer to all the chips and pretzels and onion dips as hors d'oeuvres. This will impress everyone that, even though you don't know how to cook, you do have a working knowledge of one of the Romance languages.

Do invite all your neighbors to your parties. That way they can't complain if the gathering gets too rowdy or a partygoer vomits in their front yard.

Don't feel inferior. Don't think I'm perfect. I get my clothes off the rack, too.

Catch-Alls

When I was growing up, we had what my mother called a "catch-all" drawer in our kitchen. Our house was neat and clean all around it, but that drawer was a mess—overflowing with rubber bands and torn-out recipes and clothespins and broken pencils and old calendars and incomplete decks of cards and used stamps. All you had to do was close it, though, and voila. The serenity of a well-ordered house was restored.

I think about that catch-all drawer sometimes. That is because my whole life is a catch-all container. We have catch-all drawers, pots, and bowls at my house, all teeming with stuff and papers and debris that seem to attach themselves to everyone, two- and four-footed, who lives here. The minute one of us enters the front door, we begin to shed and the catch-alls begin to fill. If I tried to close the catch-alls in my life, I'd have to shut down the whole house.

Oh, sure, I try to fight it. Once I even saw a new magazine called *Real Simple*, which seemed to be very picky about this whole pared-down, non-catch-all lifestyle. I looked at the magazine and kept wishing it would get a little pickier about its grammar, starting with its name. Then I noticed it had some kind of advice on multitasking, and I had to put it down. It's Real Simple: I almost break out in a rash every time I see words like multitasking.

The point is, I was at a low ebb like this when my husband dragged me to the mall so we could upgrade our cell phones. This supposedly had something to do with hauling ourselves into the twenty-first century and making our lives simple and easy.

So we trudge from store to store, listening to pitch after pitch. Nationwide plans! Family plans! Off-hours! Roaming charges! State of the art! Numbers of "free" minutes! Caller ID! Voice mail! We hear long, impassioned descriptions about getting plenty of minutes, since, if you go over your allotment, they evidently take your house away or something.

"We need to shop around," my husband keeps muttering, which seems a bit obsessive to me. What's wrong with him? We are not "shop-around" people by nature.

But I don't say anything, since I'm working with my own issues about sales pitches, which involves upholding my reputation as being one of the most pathetic consumers on the planet. After hearing more than two or three pitches, I immediately raise the white flag and will sign anything, mortgage my life away, just to get out of there and have people stop talking to me, begging me, smiling at me.

I also note that I have profound problems with salespeople: The more incompetent they are, the more I want to buy from them. They need my help! Give me a salesperson who stumbles and fumbles, and I'm ready to whip out my credit card. Fortunately, by that time, I am too tired to whip out anything.

So a few minutes before total collapse, we buy three phones, one for each of us and one for our son. We take them home and encode each other's phone numbers, since we can talk to each other for free. We check over the fat little reference books the company gave us, which are about the size of my car's maintenance manual.

My husband and son discover that we can send each other text messages on the phones, which are also free. My son sends me several messages a day when he gets bored at school. "Hey," they all say. He wants to know why I don't answer. I tell him that I don't consider "hey" to be a form of communication.

I look at my phone, which can add, subtract, multiply, and divide. It can be used as an alarm clock and a calendar. It takes messages and saves phone numbers and beeps a chipper tune. Too late, I realize what I've done. As usual, I haven't pared down anything in my life. I've paired up, instead, with a flashy little multitasker the size of a cashew that lights up and beeps.

Now that I think about it, it's Real Simple, unlike my life. I've added another catch-all drawer, another small corner of chaos, to my household—one that's cleverly disguised as a twenty-first-century technological convenience. Catch-alls have taken over my life and they can't be closed away or ignored, and I'm so far gone that the latest one even speaks to me. Hey, it says. Hey.

──────── ☙ ────────

Madonna Tells All

My friend Louise and I were talking about Madonna. Louise calls Madonna the trashiest entertainer she knows, and she means that as a compliment. Lately she's been trying to talk me into buying *Sex*, Madonna's new book, the one *Vanity Fair* magazine calls "perhaps the dirtiest coffee table book ever published."

"Then you could lend it to me, and I wouldn't have to spend $50," Louise says.

Ha, I thought. Why would I want to spend $50? My coffee table is dirty enough as it is.

"The book is supposed to be omnisexual," Louise continues. "What do you think they mean by that? Just think, Madonna has no sexual hang-ups at all. Can you imagine?"

"Of course she has sexual hang-ups," I say testily. "Everybody has sexual hang-ups. If she didn't, why would she be so obsessed with sex?"

"You mean you think she's frigid?" Louise asks eagerly. "Maybe she doesn't even like sex. Maybe she just talks about it for a living."

Well, if so, it's some living. This simple, midwestern girl from Pontiac, Michigan, who likes religious artifacts, Coke bottles, and guided-missile bras, has probably used up fifteen minutes of fame for every person in the Western Hemisphere.

When it comes to self-promotion, she's as tenacious as the common cold, and for some reason, she's always amused me.

Maybe Madonna is today's sex symbol, one who shows women can be as manipulative and rapacious about sex as men. Or maybe she's more than that. (After all, a group of academicians is publishing a book about her called *The Madonna Connection: Representational Politics, Subcultural Identities and Cultural Theory.*)

What's funny about Madonna, though, is how she manages to be both overexposed and little known. She flaunts her body and her omnisexual fantasies, but all we know about her, really, is what she chooses to tell us and sell us. By turns, she's a blonde, a brunette, a tramp, a virgin. Now we see her with her boy toys, now with her pastel stuffed animals. The more she changes, the more she's not the same.

Omnisexual? Who knows? Omnivorous? You bet.

You can't escape it: She's telling us more about ourselves than she is about herself. We look at her because she shows us what enthralls us, what moves us, what scares us. Looking at her, we can fantasize that—unlike the rest of us—she's completely free. Or maybe that she's just as messed-up and guilt-ridden as anyone else. Whatever the fantasy, whatever the need, she's willing to take it on and sell it to us.

And we're buying, again and again. So what if the hosts of *Entertainment Tonight* claim that we're all sick and tired of Madonna? They're wrong, that's all. You can tell me anything about Madonna, and I'd probably believe it. But don't tell me we're tired of her.

Otherwise, why would her publisher release 750,000 copies of *Sex* this week?

Why would 2 million copies of her album *Erotica* be in record stores?

And why would you have read this far?

 Chapter 7

My Favorite Governmental Bodies

The Real Marriage Penalty

A few years ago, *60 Minutes* featured a couple who got divorced every year. After they'd filed their tax returns as single taxpayers, they'd get remarried.

This saved them thousands of dollars every year because they didn't have to pay the infamous "marriage tax penalty." So they'd take a vacation somewhere in the Caribbean with all the money they'd saved, and they'd send funny little postcards to the Commissioner of the Internal Revenue Service saying things like, "Ha, ha, we're on vacation and you can't stop us."

That was how *60 Minutes* showed the couple. They were on a beach somewhere, and they were wearing bathing suits and floppy sun hats and getting really great tans and writing postcards and laughing and making fun of the IRS. All in all, they looked pretty happy and chummy, considering they'd just gotten divorced and everything.

Well, no one ever accused the IRS of being one of the many government institutions with a great sense of humor. The next thing you knew, marrying and divorcing and remarrying and re-divorcing to avoid paying the marriage penalty was declared fraudulent.

The couple would have to stay married and stay home and pay taxes like the rest of us. And stop sending cute little postcards to people who clearly didn't appreciate them.

I think about that couple every year when my husband and I pay our taxes. I've never bothered to calculate how much extra money we owe the IRS every year because we're married. (It's one of those things—like my percentage of body fat—that I don't want to know. I call this enlightened ignorance.)

Besides, I'm convinced that money isn't the only marriage penalty that's at work at tax time. April after April I realize that the greatest marriage penalty is the act of doing a joint tax return together.

We now have a CPA who calculates our taxes, but we still have to spend a long night together going over our receipts and W-2 forms and canceled checks. After ten minutes we're always surrounded by smudged carbons that have turned our fingers black and wadded-up credit card slips that have faded too much to read. We're disheveled and irritable, and we want to kill each other.

My husband, who has avant-garde notions about taxes, thinks everything should be deductible. Grocery bills, library fines, music lessons. "Are those deductible?" Speeding tickets, our cat's getting spayed, air-conditioning repairs. "Are those deductible? Well, why not? They should be."

I tell him, finally, that he's getting on my nerves with his dumb ideas, and he tells me I'm getting on *his* nerves by being rigid and unimaginative about taxes, and we stop speaking to each other for a while, which is a relief.

As the night drags on, my husband gets more and more insistent about finishing our calculations so he won't have to wreck more than one night, and all I want to do is forget about everything and go into fetal position until May.

Maybe someone should take a picture of us at this point and send it to the IRS. It's late at night and we're pale and harried and we're snapping at each other and we're buried under a growing pile of check stubs and bleached-out receipts.

So, take a picture of the marriage penalty at work, *60 Minutes*. After looking over our receipts and the taxes we owe, we won't be getting any closer to the Caribbean than this.

The IRS Speaks Softly

MEMO

To: All Americans filing joint tax returns
From: Your friends at the Internal Revenue Service

We're concerned. Somehow, we've gotten the reputation as the bad guy—the government agency that just doesn't care. We're deeply hurt by that, and we're feeling very vulnerable these days.

We were especially upset to hear so many women complaining about us in front of congressional committees in Washington. They said that filing joint tax returns with their husbands had ruined them when it turned out they owed millions of dollars in back taxes—and the IRS was, well *insensitive*, when it started freezing their bank accounts and repossessing their houses and auctioning off their minivans.

Frankly, we hated to hear that. We like to think of the IRS as the most sensitive institution in America. In fact, when we're alone in the office, we often refer to ourselves as the Big Agency With the Even Bigger Heart. (We bet you didn't know that!) We like to pretend to be tough. But believe us, we're just a bunch of softies.

That's why we want to get in touch with you at this time of year. We want to show you our sensitive side and just how much we care about our taxpayers' relationships and emotional lives.

Call us idealistic, call us hopeless romantics, but we believe that filing joint tax returns is one of the best things about being married in this great country of ours! Doing your taxes together should bring you and your mate closer together, not further apart! It's a time to turn off the television, kick back and relax while the two of you share memories, W-2 statements, and business deductions from the past year. If approached correctly, we believe that the weeks leading up to April 15 can be every bit as romantic as February 14.

So, stoke up the fire! Open a bottle of wine! Gaze deeply into each other's eyes! And start filling out your tax returns!

Since we're here to serve you, the taxpayer, and make you happier, we want to offer the following communication pointers, *Lien on Me: Romantic Tax Tips*, for all you taxpaying lovebirds out there. We're sure they will help you in your quest for a better marriage and more comprehensive tax returns:

1) If you have any criticisms of your significant other while you're filling out your return, make sure you phrase them in a constructive, nonjudgmental way. For example:

   NEGATIVE, NEEDLESSLY DESTRUCTIVE COMMENT: You're an idiot. I can't believe I married a dolt who can't even balance a checkbook. My mother was right about you.

   POSITIVE, LOVING, GENTLE CRITICISM: Why don't we have another glass of wine, snookums? Then you can tell me why you feel that burning your business-deduction slips proved your commitment to being an artist. After that, we'll put our heads together and figure out how we're going to pay thousands of dollars in extra taxes because you're such an adorable knuckle-head.

(IRS Love Tip: A gentle back rub may be appropriate at this point. Just make sure you don't have any carbon from W-2 forms smeared all over your hands.)

2) Over the course of the evening, be sure that you reaffirm your commitment to your spouse in a loving, respectful, tactful manner.

MARITAL DEDUCTION: Whatdya mean, you want me to trust your judgment and sign that return without looking at it, you big lout? I knew I should have been suspicious the minute you started taking all those trips to the Caymans and picking up a machine gun every time the doorbell rang. I want a divorce, buster.

(IRS Love Tip: Ouch! Never threaten divorce till you've finished filling out your tax return. By the way, is your spouse claiming the machine gun as a business expense? Please let us know. We'll give you confidentiality, we promise!)

MARITAL CREDIT: Of course I trust you, honey! I know I don't have a complicated financial brain like yours. But I was just curious about how we paid for our house in large, unmarked bills if we didn't have any income this year—that's all.

(IRS Love Tip: What unmarked bills?)

3) Finally, you and your spouse need to remind each other how important your marriage is. Just think! If you were single, you couldn't claim as many exemptions. We're proud to say that filing joint tax returns has saved countless marriages across the country.

(IRS Love Tip: Cut out the snickering. We can think of lots of worse reasons for staying married.)

All right, taxpayers! We hope you've enjoyed our guide to marital communications. Next year, we plan to follow it up with *Tantric Tax Returns—The Ultimate in Withholding!*

P.S. Get those returns in by April 15. And no, the wine isn't deductible.

———— ও ————

Empowering and Humanizing the IRS

WASHINGTON, D.C.—In what is clearly a devastating blow to its recent campaign to "win back the affection and admiration of the American people," the Internal Revenue Service admitted this week that Marci Keyser-Appelbaum, Ph.D., the IRS's first director of its new department of Self-Esteem and Positive Imagery, was being held by local authorities on charges of assault and battery. However, the IRS refused to confirm widespread rumors that Dr. Keyser-Appelbaum had flung a paperback copy of the tax code at B. Edward Schmidt, her immediate supervisor, requiring nineteen stitches and causing Mr. Schmidt to bleed "like corporate coffers around a presidential candidate," according to one source.

Hired only six months ago, Dr. Keyser-Appelbaum, the best-selling author of *Self Love: Having an Affair that Can Last a Lifetime!*, recently vented her frustrations with the "negative, sarcastic, nay-saying attitude that's rampant at the IRS" on ABC's *Good Morning America*. While standing on her head with co-anchor Diane Sawyer, Dr. Keyser-Appelbaum recounted how her efforts to "empower and humanize the IRS and make it lovable again" had been "brutally thwarted by the vicious, back-stabbing patriarchy at the IRS."

"I knew she had problems when she started crying and crashed onto the studio floor," Ms. Sawyer commented today. "You can tell a lot about a person by the way she stands on her head."

Among Dr. Keyser-Appelbaum's innovations at the IRS was the introduction of the 1040 tax forms in various pastel shades, accompanied by scents chosen by aromatherapy experts to "soothe" taxpayers as they filled out their returns.

"Pastels like blue and rose and green help to relax people," she explained in December, as she unveiled the IRS's "Warm and Welcoming 1040." "Filling out your tax return doesn't have to be a negative experience. Too many people had an immediate reaction of violent nausea to seeing a 1040—and we want to change that. One of our most popular scents is ginger, which calms the stomach."

Although the new "Warm and Welcoming 1040s" were greeted with universal approval—especially from the psychological, psychiatric, and self-help communities—later reports revealed widespread problems with the new forms. "People are so relaxed by the colors and fragrances that they fall asleep and don't finish their tax returns," one CPA in Dallas told *The New York Times*. "The IRS is going to have to start giving extensions for narcolepsy if they keep those forms."

In recent months, Dr. Keyser-Appelbaum's ideas were at the center of reported controversies at the agency. According to one source, her public image campaign for the agency—*The IRS: We're Just Folks Like You!*—was widely criticized and ridiculed by IRS agents.

"Somebody offered a keg of beer to anybody who could come up with the most realistic new IRS slogan," said one agency insider, who spoke on the condition of anonymity.

"There were some pretty good entries. One I remember was *The IRS: We Screw Folks Like You!* I think one of the secretaries came up with that. Somebody else suggested *The IRS:*

We Take Folks' Houses. I think that came from one of the auditors' wives. Oh, yeah, and then there was *The IRS: At Least We Aren't the IRA* and *The IRS: Don't Lien on Us, You Morons.* I'm pretty sure those came from accounting. Those nuts in accounting are always dying to do something creative for a change."

In March, Dr. Keyser-Appelbaum's public-service commercial, *Johnny and His Good Friend at the IRS,* aired nationwide. In its opening scene, Johnny, a young, freckle-faced boy portrayed by the star of *Malcolm in the Middle,* is shown with a lemonade stand under a maple tree in front of his house. An IRS agent, played by Demi Moore, drives up in a red Miata convertible to talk to him. Even though Johnny initially says he doesn't want the "mean, old government taking (his) nickels and dimes," the agent gently explains to him how important taxes are. Without his contributions, she tells him, the United States wouldn't be able to pay for schools, roads, impeachment trials, outer-space modules, and exciting wars in other countries.

In a conclusion that was termed "heartwarming" by some TV critics and "manipulative and nauseating" by others, Johnny says he wants to pay his fair share of taxes. Inside the IRS, however, one employee was quoted as saying he thought it would be a better, more effective commercial to show "big, nasty agents dressed in black, taking the little deadbeat's lemonade stand."

"Dr. Keyser-Appelbaum had a unique perspective that she shared with our agency," B. Edward Schmidt said at a press conference today. "Even though she was with us only a short while, she made an impact on all of us. Because of her, the IRS is a better place to work."

As reporters continued to question him, Mr. Schmidt playfully retorted, "Do you guys want to be audited or something?" He insisted that Dr. Keyser-Appelbaum's heaving the paperback tax code was only a friendly game of catch that IRS employees "often engage in."

Reached for comment at her suburban Washington home, where she has been released on her own recognizance, Dr. Keyser-Appelbaum would say only that she "wished the code had been hardback."

Job Advice from Monica Lewinsky

Hi! Are you totally bummed out by the job market? Are your talents, like, being underutilized? Do older women treat you like a bimbo because they're threatened by your really great $200 haircut?

I know what you're going through! That was me just a few months ago! Yes, really! I was this total sad sack who dived into the Haagen-Dazs night after night because nobody appreciated me and the contributions I was trying to make. Like I wasn't qualified to do anything important and meaningful at work!

That's when I took control of my life, and I'm here to tell you how I did it! I'm ready to answer all your questions about succeeding in the workplace and getting to the top FAST! Just write me at *Help, Monica!*

Help, Monica!—I'm so freaked out. I have a bachelor's degree from Harvard in English (summa cum laude!) and I've been working as a receptionist in a car-parts factory for the past six months. (Me! A receptionist!) To make things worse, my parents are on my back. They keep saying they paid all that Ivy League tuition for THIS? What should I do?—Heart Broken, Brain Intact

Dear Heart: I cried for five minutes after I got your letter. It's so unfair what we women have to put up with in the workplace!

Then I had to put on my eye makeup all over again, which is the time I use to think deep thoughts every day. Now I know what your problem is! All you did was tell me what college you went to and then you threw in a few foreign words so you could show off your Spanish. It was so boring that I almost fell asleep and ruined my eye makeup again.

The worst mistake you can make in a new job is to be boring! You want people to remember you, don't you? I'm talking about inner beauty, which is an important personality change that will have to come from very deep inside you. I suggest you get a good start on inner beauty the same way I did—by maxing out your credit cards at Victoria's Secret.

Help, Monica!—My mom is, like, so old-fashioned. She says if I want to succeed at work, I should wear lots of gray and brown suites with those little bow ties at the collar. What do you think?—Dressed for Excess

Dear Excess: Oh, puh-leese. I'm pretty sure it was Shakespeare who said don't put your light bulb under a bushel. What that means is that your mom is a complete antique and doesn't know what she's talking about. If a girl is going to make it in the highly competitive workplace of today, she must have the kind of wardrobe that higher-ups talk about! Please send $15.95 so you can read my new wardrobe-advice book, *Thing Me a Thong: How to Keep the Men in Your Office Humming Your Tune.* You won't believe the places a flashy wardrobe will get you!

Help, Monica!—I'm writing a term paper so I can graduate from college and become a big political success like you. Can you tell me who said, "You can never be too thin or too rich"? It's very important to the thesis of my paper.—Stuck

Dear Stuck: Oh, who cares about anybody who said something that dumb and is probably dead, anyway? I'll give you a much better quote: "You can never be too rich." Chow!

Help, Monica!—I told the professor of my Women Struggling in a Cesspool of Sexism 101 course that I thought you were a feminist because you were so empowered in the workplace. She started laughing so hard that she had an asthma attack and had to be hospitalized. After she recovered she said you were every feminist's nightmare! What do you think?—Very Confused

Dear Very: Of course I'm a feminist! I hate it when people say I'm not!

Since I'm a feminist, I hate to say bad things about other women unless I really, really have to. But all those older feminists are so ugly. I mean, hello! Who did their hair, anyway? Who dressed them?

I hate to drop names, but that was the problem with Susan Bee Anthony. If she'd been better looking, she'd be on a much better coin. (I tried all the vending machines in the White House, and they didn't even take the quarter she's on! That tells you a lot.)

Help, Monica!—How should I pick my mentor in the office? Should it be a man or a woman?—Puzzled

Dear Puzzled: I just don't know what they're teaching girls in college these days. The word is MEN-tor—and not WOMEN-tor—for lots of very good reasons I shouldn't have to explain to you.

Feeling underpaid? Unappreciated by all the meanies and creeps at your workplace? Write *Help, Monica!* to find out how to make your bosses take note of your talents!

Chapter 8

Don't Mess with My State

Stuck

Sometimes I get into these conversations with people, except they aren't really conversations. They're more like root canals and somebody forgot to give me Novocain.

"I can't believe I'm stuck in Dallas," the other person says. "I mean, have you noticed? There's no culture here."

The other person continues to talk a lot. As a rule, people like this don't expect you to say anything, since you're supposed to be struck dumb by their deep intellect and savoir-faire. You get the feeling they'd still be talking if you were a bowl of bean dip or a golden retriever.

Life is so provincial here!

Everyone's so backward! So uninformed!

The conversations are superficial and materialistic! The art's derivative!

There aren't enough hills or trees!

The winters aren't cold, and the summers are too hot!

When I bother to listen, I learn that Dallas isn't New York or San Francisco, which is always something of a shock, and it isn't close to a beach or mountains or forests. My eyes start to glaze over, and I'm sure I'm about to get the vapors, even though I've never been sure what, exactly, the vapors are.

I nod sometimes, which is what you do if you're some kind of polite social coward like me. Inwardly, though, I become

very petty and defensive, and I imagine lots of dramatic, colorful scenes that involve spilling my drink on the other person's
stuffed shirt or pouring picante sauce into his gaping mouth.
That's what happens when you're petty and defensive and
polite and cowardly all at the same time. You develop a vivid
imagination.

Which, frankly, is more than I can say for people who go
around talking like this. They completely lack imagination.
Worse, they lack curiosity. They can travel anywhere, live anywhere, but they never leave home.

Send them abroad, and they're Ugly Americans, complaining about exchange rates and suspicious-looking foreign foods
and cars that drive on the wrong side of the road. Bring them
home after a few weeks, and they've already developed Conti-
nental accents and a sniffing superiority toward the crassness
of all Americans. Bring them to Dallas, and they find me every
time.

I realize I have to stop myself in mid-ranting-and-raving to
admit that we're all capable of being guilty of this kind of myo-
pia and boorishness. We've all traveled to other cities, other
states, or other countries, inwardly ticking off the ways in
which this new locale falls short.

It's easy to be unsettled by new sights and sounds and
tastes and to miss the familiar. Why not refer back to the places
we come from to reassure ourselves—and others—who you
really are?

But you miss so much that way! If you live in Dallas and
notice only that it isn't New York or Paris, you're missing
everything. You're missing the broad sweep of the prairie and
the vivid sunsets and the steel-guitar twang of country music
and the friendliness and vitality and enthusiasm for life.

So it isn't perfect here? Find something interesting and
original to say for a change, and stop boring me with your

delusions of superiority and long, droning stories of exile among us, the culture-impaired, who talk too slow and drive too fast.

"Still Stuck in Dallas"—that's how one couple usually sign their insipid photocopied letter that, for some reason, they send to my husband and me every year. We always look over the pages and learn about the pair's trials and travails, which are invariably someone else's fault—and that someone is usually a provincial, unenlightened Texan.

"Still Stuck in Dallas," they sigh.

Uh-uh, I always think. Dallas has nothing to do with it. You're just stuck, period, hon.

The Tree in the Middle of the Street

Twenty-one years ago, when the movie *The Last Picture Show* was released, I argued with a friend about it. She said that the movie—with its doomed, bittersweet romances and its sad desolation—could have taken place anywhere in small-town America. So what if it was filmed in a dusty North Texas town? Its story was universal.

I gave up trying to convince her she was wrong. What did she know, anyway? She was from East Texas, where the trees are tall and the grass is green and the soil is black and rich. She didn't understand that *The Last Picture Show* belonged to the prairies of North and West Texas, where the wind spits dust and tumbleweeds and the horizon is flat and barren. Only there could you find the loneliness and emptiness that are as sad as the Hank Williams songs on the movie's soundtrack. Only there, I felt sure.

I knew, because I'd spent the first twenty years of my life on the Texas prairies, in places like Wichita Falls, Abilene, Midland, and Lubbock. These cities weren't as small as Archer City, where the *Last Picture Show* was filmed. But they shared the same dust storms that turned the sky red-brown, the same springtime howl of tornado sirens, and the same hard, unforgiving landscapes.

When I was a child, my father's oil company transferred our family every few years, and we'd move to a new house on the edge of one of those cities. Our new houses were called "ranch style," and they sat in the middle of a plot of cracked red clay. Here, we'd plant clumps of Bermuda grass and a few shrubs under the windows. And always, we planted a small, spindly tree that had to be staked to the ground so the wind wouldn't bend it.

A few years later, after the grass had spread and the tree was a little sturdier, we'd move again to start a new yard somewhere else. But from time to time, we'd return to drive past our old houses. "Look how green the grass is," we'd say. "And that tree. Can you believe it?" When we lived there, it was just a twig, and now it was—what?—at least ten feet tall. To think that we'd started all of this a few years ago. It was amazing to us.

I eventually left West Texas. I've lived in Florida, Virginia, California, and now Dallas, and I've seen forests and oceans and mountain ranges, dazzling autumns and springs. After all these years my eyes have changed, readjusted, and I know now that there are other landscapes and other ways of life. When my husband and I return to West Texas, as we did this summer, it looks different to me. Now it seems even flatter and more desolate and windswept than when I was a child.

Still, there's something about this land that holds me and something about it that I love. Nowhere else is there such a spectacular sweep of land and sky. Nowhere else have I found the freedom of driving on the open road, with the radio blasting and the wind blowing, and a limitless horizon in front of me.

Here, too, passing through the small towns and seeing the lonely ranch houses scattered miles apart, I feel closer to the generations that settled this land. I think about the wife of the Panhandle rancher who was so desperate for companionship that, when her husband was gone, she talked to her chickens.

Driving, I wonder why it is that I wouldn't want to live here again, and why I don't even return that often—but there's a sense that this is the place where I feel most comfortable and most at home. Maybe, I think, it's because I know this country and because I know what every bit of it—every house, every tree—has cost someone. I understand the time and hard work and optimism it took to make those small differences. In this land, everything that's green is a small victory against the odds.

"Look at that," I told my husband, as we passed through my old neighborhood in Abilene. "When they paved this street, they paved around that tree in the middle of the road, because they wanted to save it."

Looking at the tree, I could remember how wonderful it had seemed to me, as a child, that someone had wanted to spare it, even if it meant leaving it in the middle of the street. Of course, the tree seemed smaller now than it once had. But it was still green, still cutting a stark silhouette against the hot blue sky.

I knew that my husband, who's also from West Texas, understood what I was showing him. Here, in the middle of a street of aging ranch-style houses, we were looking at something beautiful.

Autumn Happened Last Thursday

Every time I hear it, I flinch.

Someone will say, with great earnestness, "You know what I really miss, living in Texas? I miss the seasons!"

Oh, brother. I try to nod wisely every time I hear that. But I worry about people like that, and I usually don't have the time to tell them everything they need to know.

You see, we do have seasons in Texas. But you're never going to understand them if you insist on pathetically clinging to traditional, storybook, New England ideals that include big trees that shed brightly colored leaves, snowstorms that howl and linger for weeks, long and glorious, blossom-ridden springs, and warm, fragrant, lazy summers that are rarely confused with sojourns in hell.

How should I say it? Seasons in that part of the world are pleasant, I'm sure. But they are so, well, *obvious*.

Not here. Understanding the seasons in Texas requires experience, subtlety, and a certain refined perceptiveness. The seasons here—with the obvious exception of summer—can be sneaky and elusive and quite short.

For example, you might find yourself wondering when it is going to be autumn. It's November, say, and where are the flawless blue skies and fresh, invigorating breezes? All of a sudden, you remember: *That's the way the weather was last Thursday*. It's not that we don't have autumn in Texas, it's just that it happened last Thursday—and you failed to realize it. Now, it's too late. Fall is over. If you missed it, it's your own fault.

Remember, you have to be alert and you have to watch carefully, very carefully. You can't afford to miss the September cool fronts when the temperature nosedives into the nineties and there is—yes!—a definite nip in the air. You can't ignore the plunge of arctic northers that titillate Texas meteorologists into dire, grim-faced warnings of ice and frozen pipes and hazardous driving conditions and salt on the roads, and spur droves of shoppers into the stores to stock up on emergency provisions like canned soup, toilet paper, and bourbon. (Some years, even the threat of icy weather is enough to be called winter.)

Whatever you do, you have to learn to be flexible. Got that? The very worst—and most potentially dangerous—way to adapt to the seasons here is simply to be very stubborn and anal about the whole thing. For example, "The calendar says it's September 22, so it must be fall, and I'm going to wear my new autumn clothes. I don't care if it is 95 degrees outside and I keel over in a heatstroke. It's fall in Boston, dammit!"

This, believe me, is the road to ruined, sweat-soaked wool clothes and an unattractive flush on your face. You might as well try to divine the seasons by watching your next-door neighbor's front porch. (You know, the one with the little Martha Stewart fixation, who hauls out the cornstalks and pumpkins every October? That's not a seasonal marker. That's an obsessive-compulsive disorder and is reportedly treatable with modern drugs and immediate withdrawal from *Martha Stewart's Living*.)

"Have you noticed," my friend Betsy remarked recently, "that the season's changing? It's getting dark earlier. And it's not as hot."

Now, some people might openly question Betsy's sanity or hint that she is hallucinating because of the triple-digit heat. Not me. Au contraire. Instead, I am impressed by her acute sensitivity to the seasons in Texas, even though she has not lived here all her life.

How long did it take? "Only four or five years," Betsy notes modestly. "A lot of it is in the nuances of the light and the way it changes. But some of it is dramatic—like the first cool front in the fall. It renews you, even though you know it's going to get hot again."

You see? All of this is hard, I know. It takes time and effort. But believe me, it is all worth it.

Because someday the rest of the world is going to turn to us, pleading for advice. What with all that global warming going on, New England's seasons are going to be a lot like ours pretty soon.

"You know what I really miss, living in New England?" they will say, and you will nod wisely, the way you always do.

Chapter 9

Traveling Lightly

Riding with the Road Warrior

I can think of two explanations for our summer vacation problems. It's either:

A. Every time we hit the city limits on a driving trip, everyone in our family goes completely nuts.

Or, B. We were nuts to take a driving vacation to begin with.

I like B. That's because it was my husband's idea to drive on this trip, and it's always nice to have someone else to blame. It would be more of an adventure to drive 2,400 miles south to Mexico, he kept saying. C'mon! Let's live a little!

But, listen. I don't think that whole seize-the-day mantra was his only reason. I think he wanted to drive because of this whole Road Warrior thing.

The minute we leave on a trip, he goes into it. Eyes locked on the horizon. Teeth clenched. Steering wheel gripped. We've got a destination, and we're going to reach it! We're not stopping for anything or anybody!

Let the Road Warrior in the driver's seat just once, and he'll hog it for the rest of the trip.

He tries to discourage me from driving on these trips, on the grounds that I honk the horn entirely too often. (This isn't true. I only honk the horn when it's absolutely necessary, so I can let other people know they've done something stupid. I think my husband's and son's rolling around in the car and saying they're so humiliated they want to die every time I honk the horn is really kind of neurotic.)

But anyway, it's a family vacation, and I decide to compromise. If he wants to drive all the time, let him. Fine. Welcome to it. I couldn't care less.

I content myself with riding shotgun and offering him constant advice about oncoming traffic and when he should pass on a two-lane road and why he should slow down. "Remember that last speeding ticket you got?" I remind him helpfully. "It cost $100."

The Road Warrior quickly develops a hearing problem. Which is just as well, because there's a lot of noise from the back seat. Our two children are surrounded by books, games, paper, and pens. They're bored, of course. This is because, to hear them talk, they are the only children in the Western Hemisphere who have to travel in a moving vehicle that doesn't have a TV and a VCR. Their parents are so old-fashioned they actually expect them to look at mountains and deserts and rivers, instead.

They start to scream and hit each other, and the Road Warrior punishes them by playing a tape of Berlioz's *Requiem* full-blast. After several minutes, I make an executive decision that I'd rather hear screaming than Berlioz, and I turn it off.

Our two children become more amiable. They start telling jokes. Most of the jokes are scatological, which they find wildly funny. They screech with laughter at their own wit.

The miles pass and the landscape whips by, and our son gets carsick several times. "I think he's going for a record," our daughter says. "This is more than he vomited at Angel Fire last year."

By the time we stop, we're hot and dusty and cramped. The back seat is littered with game pieces and gum wrappers and leaking soft-drink cans and battered magazines and books that are falling apart. Our car looks like a gerbil cage that's never been cleaned, a junkyard on four wheels.

"We made good time today," the Road Warrior crows. "Aren't you glad we didn't stop much?"

Good time? Six hundred miles, twelve hours, mayhem in the back seat, Berlioz on the stereo, a new record for carsickness, screaming brawls, and diarrhea jokes? If this is good time, never introduce me to bad.

I look into the Road Warrior's eyes and swear I can see visions of the highway staring back at me. In his mind's eye, we're still there, driving full-throttle into the distant horizon.

"I love road trips," he says, unnecessarily, and all I can think is that it's B. It's definitely B.

Disadvantage Miles

So your spouse just went platinum, huh? And you didn't?

No, we're not talking about hair here. (Ash blond is usually more flattering, anyway.) We're talking about *frequent-flier airline cards*. You know, those wonderful little platinum cards that take you to the head of the line, get you bumped up to first class, and make your self-esteem soar!

Your spouse just got one. Why didn't you?

Because, that's why. *Because* the airlines are very old-fashioned, and they have a narrow, linear worldview when it comes to frequent-flier miles. All they're interested in are trivial details such as how many miles someone has flown with their airline or which company he or she rented a car from, and so on and so on, blah, blah, blah, big deal, how boring can you get.

They don't bother to ask about *who was at home*, holding down the fort and feeding and schlepping the children and pets while your spouse was out earning those frequent-flier miles!

They don't ask about the spouse with *bags under the eyes* instead of under the arms!

They don't ask about *you*!

That's why we invented Domestic Rewards for Airline Trips by Spouses (DRATS). Founded 1997. Motto: We take the fights out of flights! We're here to make sure you—*the grounded, earthbound spouse*—get all the credit and frequent-flier miles you deserve.

Since we're such an innovative, cutting-edge company, we've designed a *new, improved system for earning miles while you're still on terra firma*. Let me explain!

To begin with, *you earn 5,000 miles each day your spouse is out of town* and you still manage to function successfully (making meals, driving car pools, and cleaning house) without the help of a straitjacket! In addition, DRATS awards bonus miles for special hardships! For example:

- *A 15,000-mile award every time your child gets sick while your frequent-flier spouse is away!* This is a special that lasts through February to take advantage of the flu season, so plan accordingly! (Please note: Stomach viruses contracted in a public place count double!)

- *A 25,000-mile bonus for every trip to the hospital emergency room!* That's right! This is your big chance! This year-round offer covers all the major sports seasons! Mega-bonus points are also available if 1) you can't find your insurance card when you get to the emergency room; 2) your child has to get stitches; 3) you have to watch while your child gets stitches; or 4) the doctor says your child is fine, but you seem to be a dithering, hysterical mess who's overreacted to a small scratch.

- *10,000 miles for every unscheduled trip to the veterinarian!* You can earn more points if your pet 1) bleeds all over your car upholstery; 2) is incontinent; 3) bites you; or 4) tries to jump out of the car when you're on the freeway.

- *5,000 miles for every deeply unsatisfactory international phone call from your spouse!* For example, aren't you tired of conversations like this:

Frequent flier: Well, we went swimming at the beach, and I got a sunburn. New Zealand has some really beautiful beaches. (Voice trails off, a bit guiltily, but not guiltily enough.) But, hey, what's been going on with you and the kids?

Frequent flier's spouse: Well, it's been cold and raining here, and Trevor got that 24-hour stomach virus and vomited all over his G.I. Joe sleeping bag, and the downstairs toilet is clogged up again, and I think I'm developing migraines. But at least my cold sore is starting to heal.

Frequent flier: Boy, this connection is bad. I can hardly hear you. I'd better go. Say hi to the kids for me!

Frequent flier's spouse: Wait a minute! I'm just getting started! Don't hang up! (garbled screams in background).

Once you have the DRATS' platinum card, you can stop all that useless screaming! You can *earn while you seethe!*

Give yourself 1,000 over-the-top bonus miles every time your spouse calls from an exotic location and uses some weak excuse to try to get off the phone before you've told him about how the cat fell out of a tree and is under suicide watch at the vet's!

Grab another 5,000 miles every time your spouse pretends your call was "disconnected"!

Glom on to still another 10,000 miles if your spouse is calling from another hemisphere and you haven't made it out of your bathrobe all day!

All right already! It's time to add up those miles and collect those platinum cards you've been earning! Remember, if you request it, your children can use your frequent-flier miles, too! Wouldn't it be fun to surprise your spouse the next time he thinks he's going out of town by himself?

Carefully Wrapped Packages

The first time I saw Masao and Yumi, they were slumped in a van in front of our house. It was August, and they were limp from the fierce Texas heat and semiconscious with jet lag.

"I think they need to sleep," said one of my husband's graduate students, who had picked them up at the airport. "They're exhausted."

We unloaded the two of them and their luggage from the van and led them up to our daughter's room so they could sleep. Two days later they reemerged, brighter-eyed and energetic, ready to tackle a new country.

They had come from Kyoto to Dallas for a year so Masao could work with my husband on his psychological research and Yumi could improve her English. They were a young couple in their late twenties, earnest and gracious and eager to please. It was impossible not to be charmed by them—even if we spent most of our time communicating with extravagant gestures and repeated words.

After Masao and Yumi moved to their own apartment, I saw them every two or three weeks at parties and holiday gatherings. By the spring their English had improved remarkably. They loved Dallas, they both said enthusiastically, and they loved the United States and all the friends they had made here.

Masao, in particular, had become almost dangerously enthusiastic. He was especially fond of our custom of hugging close friends. When he came to parties, he gave his friends big, overwhelming bear hugs. Some nights you could almost hear ribs crack all over the room.

"You know what I want?" Masao said. It was early that summer, shortly before they left to go back to Japan. "I want to be a more sensitive person," he said. "More emotional, like American men."

As sensitive and emotional as American men? "Mmmmmm," I said. I nodded over and over in what I hoped was an encouraging, nonjudgmental way. I tried to look as serious as he did. "Mmmmmm."

Masao and Yumi returned to Japan, and we didn't see them till May three years later. Masao and his university invited my husband to speak at two conferences, and I came along, too. While they talked about research night and day, I wandered around the streets of Kyoto, intrigued by the simple beauty the Japanese created in the smallest ways. Packages were wrapped carefully, precisely. Paintings and décor were exquisitely spare. Food was artfully layered and displayed. I could never be Japanese, I realized. I was far too messy and careless, too American.

For eight days, Masao and Yumi escorted us around their country. They were always thoughtful, always concerned whether we were having a good time, always showing that same sweetness and graciousness they had evinced in our own country. One night at dinner, I told the story of Masao's wanting to be as sensitive as American men—and how American women found that hilarious, since we don't think our own men make a dent on the sensitivity scale. Masao beamed when I told the story. "You think I'm sensitive," he said. "I will tell that to Yumi. She doesn't think I'm sensitive at all."

We spent three days in Tokyo then returned to the slower pace of Kyoto. Our last full day, we went to Hiroshima, which was less than two hours away on a Japanese bullet train. We took a taxi to the museum and walked from exhibit to exhibit with other tourists. There were photographs and displays of the devastation of the atomic bomb, scenes of rubble and bodies mutilated and strewn in the debris. Here and there were a few shattered watches and clocks, all of them stopped at the minute the bomb exploded at 8:15 in the morning.

English translations of the exhibits were carefully worded. The surprise attack on Pearl Harbor "hurtled" Japan into the war, one of them said. The sentence was insistently passive; there was no cause, only effect.

Why had the United States dropped the atomic bomb? another display queried. The answers were laid out, one by one: To end the war quickly; to limit American casualties inevitable in an invasion of Japan; to prevent the intervention of the Soviet Union.

Like all the other displays, this was flat and impassive. The passions were limited to the walls of postwar letters from Hiroshima mayors, vehemently protesting other nations' developing and testing their arsenals of nuclear weapons.

After a couple of hours, we left the museum with Masao, Yumi, and Hiroko, a graduate student, and walked to a nearby restaurant. We had seen too much. What could we say? Nothing. We were all silent.

Sitting in the restaurant, we began to talk very tentatively. My husband asked whether the three of them blamed the American people for dropping the atomic bomb, and they said no. They didn't see any use for guilt on either side, for a reexamination of the past. They wanted to talk about what we could do for the future.

Masao, Yumi, and Hiroko talked about seeing exhibits of letters from kamikaze pilots. These were boys and men who died in the war, they said, calling for their mothers. It was heartbreaking to read their letters. I shifted on the cushion and listened impatiently. These were also boys and men who fought against boys and men in my parents' generation, and I wasn't sure I wanted to hear their stories. Of course they were young. Of course they were innocent and emotional. Of course it was all a tragedy.

But they had died on the wrong side of a war whose justice I had never questioned. I could object to the War in Vietnam or World War I, but not the Second World War. In my family and even in my generation, wasn't this war—our last "just" war—beyond discussion?

"What you have to understand," I said, "is that Pearl Harbor is as emotional a topic to Americans as Hiroshima is to Japan." And Japan hadn't been hurtled into the war, I added silently. It had hurtled itself.

Our three Japanese friends nodded. They told us how history is taught in Japanese schools—a procession of names and dates, battles and wars, and victories and defeats, much like the displays in the Hiroshima museum. How much was Japan at fault for World War II? They didn't know, really. They had been told that Japan had attacked Pearl Harbor to fend off American aggression in Asia. How could they know what to believe?

American aggression in Asia? Oh, come on. I wanted to tell them what had happened, tell them everything I'd grown up knowing all my life and had never questioned. But I didn't. What good would it have done?

Instead, I asked whether Japan, like Germany, had been working on the atomic bomb at the same time the Americans had. No, they said. What I wanted to ask, but didn't, was a question the museum hadn't posed: If the Japanese had possessed the atomic bomb before the Americans did, would they have used it on us? I felt sure I knew the answer. They would have used it if they had had it—the same way we did. It was wartime, and wars are horrific.

The conversation dwindled to a halt, until we began to talk about other, safer topics. We were back on familiar ground. We were friends again.

Should we have continued to talk about something this painful, buried in our collective pasts? Should I have questioned my own belief that the atomic bomb had been terrible, but necessary, a quicker end to a war our country hadn't started? I don't know. What did this war have to do with the five of us, sitting at a table together more than fifty years later? Maybe those were questions and answers that belonged to another generation, and not to us.

Looking across the table, I saw faces I admired and had grown to love. I realized how much I didn't want to hurt them. What could be more important than that?

The next day our plane lifted away from the airport, and I watched Japan disappear into the ocean behind us. We'd visited a country that values beauty and serenity, agreement and politeness, a country that drapes a bland cloak of forgetfulness over its dark, unexamined history. We had left friends there. Now we were being hurtled back into our own sprawling, messy country. But, even here, we have our own precisely wrapped packages, given to us by people we trust. Sometimes we open them. Sometimes we don't.

Chapter 10

All Work

I Don't Get Tough, Mr. Gittes

Four months ago, we buy a new computer, since my old one is making noises like someone gagging on throat lozenges. "I strongly recommend a three-year warranty," the salesman says. "We'll come and fix it at your house. *On-site service.* You don't want to have to mail your computer in to be fixed, do you?"

No, I don't. Au contraire. My husband immediately begins to grumble about how warranties are useless, so I gouge him in the ribs with my elbow. Of course I want on-site service! I'm a savvy consumer, right? Sold!

My computer and I are very happy in our first few days together. Then it starts dumping me off the Internet. "Goodbye!" it says rudely, whipping me out of cyberspace and depositing me on terra firma. Sometimes it even repeats itself—*Goodbye!*—as if I haven't gotten the hint.

I call the Internet people ("the provider"). We make lots of adjustments to my computer. (I say "we." They tell me everything to do, and I obey slavishly, like one of Pavlov's drooling dogs.) Nothing helps.

I call the computer company's ("the manufacturer") help line. "We" also make adjustments to my computer. This is what's called *troubleshooting*, I soon learn. The basic premise of troubleshooting, I further learn, is that the customer is always an idiot.

Time passes. The manufacturer blames the provider and the provider blames the manufacturer, and they both say it might be the phone line. No, I say patiently, it couldn't possibly be the phone line, since we tested our other computer on it.

I have to explain this a lot, since every time I call, I get a new person at the manufacturer's number who asks the same questions and makes the same suggestions. I now have my own case number, but each call is tabula rasa. I spend hours— *days? weeks?*—on hold, listening to bad music and intermittent voices raving about what a great company the manufacturer is. We talk. We troubleshoot. We commiserate. Nothing helps. I'm still being dumped off the Internet. *Goodbye!*

Finally, the manufacturer agrees I need a new modem. The latest voice tells me where I can drop off my computer to be worked on. Forget it, I say smugly. I have an on-site warranty. (Yippee! Vindication! This is what happens when you're a savvy consumer!)

A long silence. You must have a warranty with the computer store, the manufacturer's voice says.

I call the computer store ("the store"). The store tells me that my on-site warranty doesn't begin till my one-year warranty with the manufacturer expires. In the meantime, I'll have to drop off my computer to be worked on. I become irate. I mention words like *false premises* and *misleading*. Why would I have bought a warranty under those circumstances? I wouldn't have. The store gets back on the line and says it will make an exception in my case.

The store installs a new modem. It works, sort of—if you have a lot of time on your hands. I could get a personal makeover in the time it takes to get on the Internet. Maybe liposuction, even. I'm convinced I've been given a nineteenth-century modem, the wagon train special.

So now I have a dilemma. When I'm not on the phone, troubleshooting, I have a life—a novel due in two weeks and a husband and children who are always due for something. Do I want to spend the rest of my days on the phone, complaining to nameless, faceless people and leading them through my tortured Internet saga once more?

I write a pointed letter to the manufacturer's president, demanding satisfaction, and send it certified mail. I send a copy to my friend Pat, who's a lawyer.

A few days later I get a call from a woman with a soothing voice and a name like a rock star. She's with the manufacturer's customer relations department. "We're going to take care of this problem," she says. (We!) She sounds very nice. In fact, she's so nice, she even ends her voice-mail greeting with "Have a blessed day."

Another new modem is installed. It still doesn't cut it. *Goodbye!* The man who installs the modem says he'd get a new computer if he were me. There's clearly something wrong with this baby, he says.

The woman with the name like a rock star stops taking my phone calls. "Have a blessed day," her recorded voice croons again and again. She doesn't return my messages, either.

So here I am. A savvy consumer, trying to get satisfaction. It's a full-time job and—trust me on this—it doesn't pay well.

Ditched by the Internet. Waiting by the phone. Gnashing my teeth. Watching life and cyberspace pass me by. Sounding more and more like a bad country-and-western song.

All of this makes me think of a line from *Chinatown* that I've always loved and wanted to say. "I don't get tough, Mr. Gittes," Faye Dunaway purrs. "My *lawyer* does."

Well, I don't get tough, either. But I think Pat has real potential in that department.

Goodbye! And please—have a blessed day.

Rejection Builds Character

Face it. Your failure to be chosen for Oprah Winfrey's book club isn't the source of your deep-seated problems. If you were an emotionally healthy person, you wouldn't be a writer in the first place. You'd be something normal.

But no. You want to spend your life hunched in front of a computer screen. Most days the computer screen is blank, because a) you turned it on only three hours ago, and you're still waiting to get in the mood; b) you got in the mood, but it was the wrong one; or c) you wrote something that was so spectacularly bad that you had to delete it and you're now completely demoralized.

Other days, though, you fill your computer screen. Pages flow and overflow like dazzling spring creeks. You decide you're brilliant. (Gifted!) You fall in love with yourself all over again. You adore being a writer! How could you ever think of doing anything else? No way! This is where you belong.

Uh-oh. Do you hear something going *splat*? It's the sound of your former ego, breaking like a raw egg. You're an omelet tartare. Editors say no, thanks. Sometimes, they just say no. Your agent says forget it. Even your friends say, well, it isn't your best work. So does your spouse, whom you currently aren't speaking to because of his total insensitivity to your needs.

You brood and sulk. You quit writing for 24 hours. (No one notices.) You recover, sort of. You decide that, on the whole, rejection is good. It will make you stronger. That's right, stronger! Easy success makes people flabby and superficial. Not you. You'll write about something deep and meaningful. (Like rejection, for instance. The angst of rejection.)

You write more. You write a book. Your spouse, whom you have recently forgiven, likes it. So do your friends, your agent, and an editor. It's published. You're wildly happy, ecstatic, exuberant.

Until you come to a new realization. Which is that being published makes you even less emotionally healthy, if that's possible.

You find yourself lurking around bookstores. You ask, very casually, if they have your book. When they don't, you shake your head sadly and say, Well, you've heard the book is very, very good, and isn't it a shame this bookstore doesn't have high literary standards. If the clerk asks whether you want to special-order the book, since it's so wonderful, you make some kind of pathetic excuse so you won't have to admit you're the author.

If the bookstore carries your book, this means you will patronize and lurk around the store for the rest of your life. You also have work to do. You have to make sure the store is displaying your book correctly, with its cover out, preferably at eye level. If not, you may have to do a little shelf-arranging. It's a lot of work, but you don't mind.

You gratuitously bring up your book in conversations with complete strangers, because you have no pride. You agonize about reviews. You obsess about sales.

Just when you're at your most vulnerable, you hear about the monthly book club on Oprah's show. You read that once a book is selected for her show, it automatically sells hundreds of thousands of copies. Authors become incredibly successful and rich.

You think about what you'd do if Oprah called you. You imagine how well—how gracefully!—you'd handle sudden fame. It wouldn't change you at all.

The phone doesn't ring, and you recall that, on the whole, rejection is good. Rejection builds character. The angst of rejection. The angst of rejection by Oprah.

Somewhere, nearby, you can hear something going *splat!* Someone must be making an omelet.

Survival Tips for the Book Festival World

I went to the Texas Book Festival last weekend. Naturally.

That's because I love the Texas Book Festival. It's my idea of heaven, going from room to room and hearing wonderful writers talk about their books and readers asking questions and watching people get excited about the written word.

Besides all of that, I was there because they invited me. When you're a writer, you usually go every place you are invited, especially when people are nice to you and you get free food and, for a few days, you actually get the most price-less commodity in Austin, which is good parking.

But it's also a funny business, being a featured author. You spend most of your life isolated from humanity, staring at a computer's blank screen and—let's face it—becoming a little bit wild-eyed and twitchy. And then somebody invites you somewhere nice where you're expected to be clean and pre-sentable and somewhat sociable. I speak from personal experience on this one. I can usually spend a day or two imper-sonating an extrovert at these gatherings, but then I collapse into some kind of semi-coma and somebody has to put me in a corner and water me several times a day till Christmas.

But trust me on this one. These festivals can be fun, as long as you have the right attitude of not taking yourself too seri-ously. Did you get that? *Not taking yourself too seriously?* No, I didn't think you did.

Perhaps I should expound:

1) There will be bigger names than you at the festival—
   writers who have sold a gazillion books and won prizes
   with flashy, meaningful words like National Book Award
   or Pulitzer attached, prizes you'd probably auction off
   your firstborn to win, but nobody's asked you yet. Get
   used to it, and try not to drive yourself batty by making
   constant comparisons, such as:

   a) How a certain writer is holding court in a room as
      big as a medium-sized ranch, which is packed to the
      eaves with slavishly adoring fans who want to bask
      in the presence of literary genius and buy as many
      books as possible, and here you are, speaking in a
      modest-sized room where the panel outnumbers
      the tiny audience of family members and a few close
      friends you have sworn you will track down and dis-
      member if they don't show up at your reading, along
      with a small number of lost souls who look dazed
      and bewildered and may, in fact, believe your pre-
      sentation is part of their guided tour of the state
      capitol.

      I speak from personal experience on this one, as
      well, having gone mano a mano with Frank McCourt
      two years ago, although I'm not sure Frank was
      aware of the intense competition. I stared out at the
      audience and told myself what a good opportunity
      this was to improve my sense of humor, even
      though I could have sworn I had a pretty good sense
      of humor to begin with;

   b) How you're sitting at an autograph table, next to
      someone so wildly popular that her line of devotees
      stretches to the river, but the only person who
      approaches you wants to know if you can give him

directions to the closest vegetarian restaurant where they make their own tofu from scratch. In extreme situations such as this, you should either: take up meditation very quickly; reassure yourself in a passive-aggressive way that is completely beneath you that the writer next to you must have an empty, meaningless life that she tries (unsuccessfully!) to fill with overwhelming book sales, money, and the adoration of her public and that someday we'll all be dead, anyway, so what difference does it make?; and/or give the vegetarian precise directions to the nearest barbecue joint where the cook is an escaped convict named Butch.

2) Expect anything to happen when you put a bunch of writers together on stage. For example, I've been witness to:

a) a panel where three writers were to share time equally. Unfortunately, though, the first writer took it upon herself to read her entire book (a children's picture book, but *still*) and hog almost all the allotted time for the entire panel, while the moderator and two other writers looked on in quiet horror;

b) a panel at a statewide library meeting where the first writer read a passage from her most recent novel that described, in less-than-flattering detail, a high school football coach who was attempting to teach world history. The writer read aloud a scene where one student whispered to another that the coach "taught world history because he was too dumb to teach algebra. He kept looking at all the x's in the equations and wondering why they were using his signature over and over in a math problem."

All of which everyone thought was pretty funny, till the second writer got up for her presentation and happened to mention she was married to a high school football coach.

So, there you are. On panels—as in life—be careful what you read. Once again, I speak from personal experience.

Mr. Smith's Wife

I'd like to say that all the years I spent in higher education taught me everything I know. But it isn't true. The year I was a secretary was the most educational of my life.

That year, I learned: 1) Secretaries run the country; 2) Lots of them have more on the ball than their supervisors; and 3) I was a horrible secretary.

I learned all of this the year I was twenty-two. I'd just graduated from college with a degree in comparative literature, which meant that I could read books in two foreign languages, as long as they were written at a kindergarten level. That was nice, but it didn't pay the rent in any language.

So I went to work as a secretary for a small law firm. It was my first real job, and I wanted to do well. I wanted to learn all about the business world and law and human relationships in the workplace. It would be great experience, I felt sure.

I was the secretary for Mr. Seymour, who was one of the two lawyers, and I also served as a receptionist and answered the phone for both him and Mr. Smith, the other attorney. I didn't see much of Mr. Smith, an older man. Fortunately, his secretary was happy to tell me all about him.

"Mr. Smith thinks he's a ladies' man," she said. "He's so vain he even takes off his glasses when he's talking on the phone to a woman."

Every Christmas, she said, Mr. Smith sent her to the bank to get crisp, new $100 bills to give all his girlfriends. She said she always made it a point to ask the bank to give her wadded-up, dirty bills.

"He's married, isn't he?" I asked.

"Yes, but no one's ever seen his wife," she said.

The days passed. I typed and took shorthand and answered the phone and listened to the Watergate hearings and thought about my future. Most of the time, I also waited for something interesting to happen. Surely the workplace was more dynamic than this, I kept thinking.

I was alone in the office late one afternoon when an elderly woman came in. She wore a wig of apricot-colored curls that sloped a little too far to the right, and she had bright spots of rouge on her cheeks. After we'd talked for a few minutes, she told me she was here to see Mr. Smith.

"I'm Mrs. Smith," she said.

I couldn't believe it. I was the first person in the office to meet Mrs. Smith! Wait till I told the other secretaries!

"It's nice to finally meet you," I said. "Mr. Smith should be back soon."

A few minutes later, Mr. Smith called.

"Guess who's here," I said. "Your wife is waiting to see you."

"My wife?" Mr. Smith said. "She never comes to the office."

"Well, she's here now," I said. "I'll put her on the line."

The Smiths talked for a few minutes. Then she hung up the phone and told me goodbye and left.

The next morning I was at work bright and early, as usual. Mr. Smith came in a few minutes later. He didn't look quite as friendly as usual.

He walked straight to my desk. "That wasn't my wife at the office yesterday," he said. "That was my mother. Good God—Mother's almost eighty." He whipped off his glasses and glared at me. "How old do you think I am, anyway?" he said.

Uh-oh.

"Well, not very old," I said tactfully. Mr. Smith jammed his glasses back on and marched into his office.

After that, I felt, the bloom was off the rose. I stayed at the law firm for a few more months, but Mr. Smith was never quite as friendly as he'd been before. When I turned in my resignation in May, it was funny. Both Mr. Smith and Mr. Seymour hid their disappointment quite well.

Twenty years and several jobs later, I realize there are three morals to this story: 1) Introduce your husband, wife, and parents at the office so there won't be any mistaken identities; 2) Take your secretary out to lunch next Wednesday for Secretaries Day; and 3) As long as you're at it, make it a nice lunch and remember how lucky you are. After all, you could have had me as your secretary.

Temporary Help

I saw the movie *Clockwatchers* with my husband. He liked it, but he didn't squirm with recognition nearly as much as I did.

So I went back to see it again with my friend Betsy, and we groaned and gritted our teeth and practically threw ourselves on the floor. Like the four women in the movie, Betsy and I had been temporary clerical workers when we were younger. If we'd forgotten anything about those experiences, the movie reminded us.

Watching the clock as it crept toward 5 o'clock.

Filing.

Having to "look busy" when you had nothing to do.

More filing.

Answering the phone when you didn't know anything about the company or what it did or who worked there.

"I want you to answer the phone in a loud, strong voice," said the man who owned the investment company where I worked when his secretary was on vacation. It was the summer of 1971 or 1972, and I was in Florida, and I was wilting. That's what happens when the temperature and humidity are in the triple digits, and you're from West Texas. You wilt. (What did he mean, a loud, strong voice? I could hardly breathe.)

"A loud, strong voice shows confidence in our company," the man said. He looked at me doubtfully. "You got that?"

I said yes, I did. Which is what you do when you're a temporary worker. You go around acting like you know what you're doing, even when you can't remember the name of the company you're working for.

The morning passed slowly. Every time I answered the phone, I practically screamed into it to show how much confidence I had in the company. I didn't think that was a very nice way to answer the phone, if you wanted my opinion, but that was what this guy said he wanted.

I was on the phone when the guy left the office. He mumbled something to me about lunch and about locking the door, and then he disappeared. When I went out for lunch, I closed the door carefully, just the way he'd told me.

An hour later, I came back. The guy was on the floor, kneeling in front of the door. He seemed awfully tense and grumpy.

"Is anything wrong?" I asked.

He glared at me. "I told you to leave the door unlocked so I could get back in," he said. "Now, we're locked out."

I could hear the phone ringing behind the locked door. But that's all I can remember. I guess we probably got back into the office eventually, but I'm not sure how. But I do recall that this guy didn't need my help again the next day, for some reason.

"One summer I had a job in a jewelry store," Betsy whispered. "I had to polish silver every day and get that goo all over my hands. One of the old ladies who worked there always pointed out spots I hadn't shined well enough. 'You missed a place, dear'—that's what she'd tell me." Betsy made a big face and a gagging noise.

It was all there in *Clockwatchers*. The office busybody who tells you your hem is dragging. The long, echoing halls full of metal file cabinets. The people who never bother to learn your name. The endless forms you have to type and retype. The temporary workers who don't stand up for each other because they need the work and good references.

Watching all of that, I recalled a time in my life when my future stretched ahead of me like a broad, blank canvas, and I had all the time in the world. Until I saw *Clockwatchers*, some kind of perverse nostalgia had turned those temporary-work memories pastel and pleasant and dreamily blurred; if you can get nostalgic about leisure suits, I suppose you can get nostalgic about anything if you're deluded enough.

After seeing the movie twice, I thought about all those temporary summer jobs I had when I was part of a world nobody pays much attention to—faceless workers who seem interchangeable and get too little respect. The funny thing is, even though you're sometimes treated badly, you aren't completely powerless. Temporary workers can always protest in very small ways that no one ever knows about.

"If you want to make something disappear, just file it wrong," says one of the characters in the movie.

And, "Hang up on people. If it's really important, they'll call back."

And, "Give lots of advice. By the time they realize it's wrong, you'll be gone."

And, "Lock somebody out of his office and pretend it was a great big accident"? Well, maybe, now that you mention it. We'll call it temporary insanity.

Chapter 11

Too Damned Many Growth Experiences

The Fortune Cookies

Symbols and signs. My husband tells me I see too many of them wherever I look. But I can't help it.

I find a penny on the sidewalk, and who cares if it isn't worth anything these days? It means I'm going to have a lucky day.

I like fortune cookies, too. "Wealth awaits you real soon"—that's what my all-time favorite fortune cookie told me. So what if it was ten years ago? Maybe fortune cookies have a long-term version of what "real soon" is. I can be patient when we're talking about wealth.

Normally, and like most people, I don't take these superstitions to extremes. They're diversions, that's all.

But then, sometimes your life changes on you—veering off course suddenly and dramatically—and you start taking everything to extremes. In your heart, you always knew you never had total control over your life. But now you don't even have the illusion of control.

Last week, when my own life veered out of control, all those small signs and symbols and superstitions began to take on much greater significance. I found myself looking everywhere for something hopeful that would tell me everything was going to be all right.

I had lunch with my friend Laurie after I'd gotten a series of bad reports from mammograms, magnifications, and ultrasound tests. At the end of the meal, the waiter brought us two fortune cookies wrapped in plastic.

"You choose first," Laurie said, and I did. I shut my eyes and chose a cookie and broke it open. "Nothing very bad is going to happen to you," it said. Ordinarily, I'd call that a pathetic fortune—I wanted wild, extravagant promises of success and happiness. That day, though, it meant something good to me. Maybe, I thought, it was referring to my upcoming biopsy.

A few days later my husband and I went to an open house at our daughter's middle school, and I wore my favorite earrings. To me, they're beautiful—long, gold-colored rectangles—and whenever I wear them, I feel good.

It was about an hour later, as we traipsed down the hall, that I noticed my left earring was gone. My husband and I searched for it, retracing our steps up and down the hallways. But we couldn't find it. At that point, it was more than losing one of my favorite earrings. It was a sign of something bad to come.

The day after I heard that the biopsy had shown malignancies, my friend Janet called from Santa Fe, and we talked and cried together over the phone. "Can I bring you something back from here?" she asked.

At first I couldn't think of anything. Then I realized what I wanted. "There's something you can do for me," I said, and told her about the earrings. "I want my earring replaced."

When I said that, I realized how much my life had changed. I knew it was time for me to be more willing to ask for help and to accept it. I thought, too, about my still-ridiculous search for meaning in small signs. Maybe, as I'd done with the earrings, sometimes you could take a sign you'd gotten—or an unwanted course your life had taken—and change it and bend it to your will and make it better. Sometimes you could and sometimes you couldn't, and I was going to have to learn the difference.

That night I went outside into our backyard and stared up at one of the most beautiful skies I've ever seen. The moon was bright and white-silver, surrounded by a corona of ice-blue clouds. I looked up at that radiant sky, and for a few seconds, I wondered if it could be a sign of something good about my future.

Then I realized I was searching for signs when I already had a clear meaning right there, immediate and in front of me. I'd been given a glimpse of pure beauty that I had to seize and hold close, and I had to be grateful I'd had it for even a few brief moments.

The Words We Remembered

Everything happens for a reason, a friend told me a few months ago. There must be a reason I got cancer, she said, even if I didn't realize it yet.

"I don't believe that," I told her.

I look around and see a more unreasonable, random world than she does. But that doesn't mean I'm not trying to understand it. It's just that I think I have to provide my own reasons and define life in my own way.

So I had cancer and surgery and chemotherapy and radiation. At times I've been scared to death, and I don't think that fear ever leaves completely. I cried and I worried and I despaired, and some days I was a real mess.

All of this is true. But it's only a part of what happened. What's also true is that my family and friends were wonderful and warm, my doctors were bossy but superb, and everybody looks bad in hospital dressing gowns. Maybe I've never cried as much in my life, but I've never laughed as much, either.

"Have you vomited yet?" my nine-year-old son kept asking me after my chemo treatments. When he sees movies, he wants car chases and fiery wrecks and Uzis; when his mother gets medical treatment, he wants action and drama. I told him about the great new anti-nausea drugs these days, and he looked disappointed. "Have you vomited yet?" he asked me again the next afternoon.

Sitting around with other patients in waiting rooms, I exchanged stories and family pictures and made new friends in that quick way you can when someone's going through the same thing you are.

Inside doctors' offices, nurses gave me brochures with the doctors' photos and information about their education and families and even their hobbies. (Their *hobbies?* Now, wait a minute. The more I thought about it, the more I realized *I didn't want my doctors to have hobbies*. I wanted them to spend 24 hours a day thinking about my case.)

Thanksgiving and Christmas passed, and the morning of our wedding anniversary, my husband and I tried to elbow each other out of the way so we could brush our teeth in the sink.

"We've been married twenty-three years," I said, speaking to his reflection in the mirror. "After all that time—who would have guessed we'd both be bald?"

But that's what was strange. In the midst of the fear and uncertainty, I've never felt as completely alive in my life. There was a clarity I'd never had before, a sense of what was important and what wasn't.

The months after my diagnosis were the most terrible and frightening and wonderful of my life, and I never want to forget what I've been through.

I still don't think serious illness happens for a reason. I do think we have to grasp the very worst events and wring out every scrap of meaning and feeling and hope we can find. I think we have to savor those small, dazzling bursts of joy that come out of the darkness.

That's what happened to us the day it snowed and iced over and the schools closed. It was the day we heard that Gene Kelly had died, and again and again on television, we saw his famous scene from *Singing' in the Rain*.

That evening my husband and children and a friend and I walked to a nearby restaurant. The sky was dark and the streets were slick and shiny and only a few cars slid past. Along the sidewalks and through the parking lots, my husband and I danced and sang the melody from the movie and pirouetted slowly in the ice. Our children looked mortified, and my husband noted that it was too bad we didn't know the words to the song.

But it was all right. We remembered the line about how we were happy again.

The Waiting Room

The man is in his fifties or sixties, dressed in a pair of faded denim overalls. He rocks back and forth nervously while he speaks to the nurse at the front desk. He hums tunelessly. He's loud and he talks too much.

"He's whistling in the graveyard," my husband says, noticing my growing irritation. "He's scared to death."

"I'm here to give someone a ride," the man tells the nurse. "I'm not a patient here," he adds quickly.

That does it. I hate this man—*this big oaf*—I decide quickly. If he doesn't shut up, I may have to strangle him. I'm usually not the violent type, but today I'm feeling volatile and out of control. The police will come and they'll have to pry my hands off his neck. It will be very messy and illegal, and I'll have to go to prison or something.

Usually, as I say, I'm not like this. I like to think of myself as a compassionate, tolerant person. But on days like this, when I'm in the oncology waiting room, my compassion shrivels. It's been exhausted by my own terror and the strength of my feelings for the other patients in this room and those who love them. Outside this small, intense, frenetic circle of emotion, my tolerance withers to almost nothing.

"Got any *Playboy* magazines in this waiting room?" the man asks the nurse. She says no, and I immediately begin to fantasize about having a black belt in karate. Today a lethal weapon might come in handy. When you're a feminist and you've had a bilateral mastectomy and you're waiting to have blood drawn to see if you're still cancer-free after three years, you don't think it's cute or charming when some Neanderthal cracks a joke about *Playboy*. Who does this guy think he is—the president?

The man continues to hum some idiotic song, and, as always, I sit and watch others in the waiting room. I can't help myself. I want to know their stories. I want to reach out to them, to touch them, to smile and offer encouragement. We're together somehow, sitting in this room where fear hovers like an invisible fog, wrapping itself around us, squeezing us roughly. We're together somehow, but we're also isolated from one another, trapped inside different bodies with different diagnoses and different futures. We sit together in the waiting room, but the news we hear from our doctors is individual.

In the chair across from us, a woman about my age is red-eyed and weeping. She's sitting next to a young man—her son, clearly—who's reading a magazine. She must have just gotten a bad diagnosis, I decide. But minutes later, I see I'm wrong. A technician calls a name for blood work, and a pretty blond woman in her twenties stands up and touches the middle-aged woman as she passes. The woman isn't crying for herself, I now realize; she's crying for a daughter who isn't much older than mine.

A technician calls my name and painlessly takes blood from my arm. I think about my friend Kathy, whose veins were scarred by chemotherapy. Every year at her checkup, she terrorizes the technicians. "You only get to stick me once," she tells them. "If you can't do it right the first time, find someone who can." Maybe, if I work hard at it, I can learn to scare people the way Kathy does. It sounds better than being scared all by yourself.

"How do you feel?" That's what my oncologist always asks. It sounds like a trick question to me. Today I snap and ask why doesn't *he* tell *me* how I feel. He's the expert, isn't he? After all these tests, doesn't he know more about me than I know about myself? He flinches, and I apologize, because he's a good, caring person and I like him a lot.

"I just get so scared at these checkups," I say, because sometimes I get exhausted by acting brave and cracking bad jokes like that idiot in the waiting room. I've loved and respected my doctors, but I'm tired, too, of giving myself over to these people in white coats with their relentless, guarded eyes and vicious tests that pry secrets out of my body and their arsenal of space-age machinery.

Sometimes, too, I feel as if it's my mission in life to talk about my fear—that unspeakable emotion—to yank it out of the dark corners of my heart and see if it shrinks in the light. I want my doctors to know how scared I am, and I want to tell them about the terror that sweeps over me and ravages me and changes me so completely that for a few days, I'm not myself, I'm not the person I want to be. I want them to understand me better. I want them to understand the patients who are still in that waiting room today and in the days and years to come.

My oncologist tells me I'm doing fine. He says he'll see me again in six months. Then he shakes my hand and sends me back into the world outside that waiting room. I plan to stay there as long as I can.

———— 🍎 ————

Chase Keller (1982-2000)

Our upstairs phone wasn't working, and we could barely hear the phone downstairs when it began to ring. It was five in the morning, and our room was dark and cold; it was too much trouble to go downstairs. So my husband and I lay in bed and listened to the phone ring, quietly and insistently. After a few rings, it was answered by our voice mail, and the house was quiet again.

Two hours later my husband went downstairs to check the voice mail. By then the sky had lightened outside our windows and the day was beginning. "You need to listen to the message," he said. "Something's happened. But I don't know who it is."

He handed me the phone he'd brought upstairs, and I listened to the message. It was a friend calling to tell me her teenage son had committed suicide the evening before. Her voice broke then it continued. "I'm just sitting here in the wee, small hours of the morning," she said. "Please call me."

Her son. Her eighteen-year-old son.

When I called my friend, her voice was soft and dazed. I listened to her—what else could I do? I wanted so badly to be able to do something more, to take her pain for a few minutes or a few days, and divide it, somehow, among the people who cared about her. Couldn't I do that? Couldn't I do something? No, I couldn't. In the face of such devastating grief, I could only listen and say how sorry I was.

I know this woman because we're both breast cancer survivors, both involved in a local resource center for survivors. But we know each other better than that, because she'd asked me for advice about her son when he became depressed three years ago. She asked me because my husband is a psychologist, but also because she knew I'd suffered from severe depression in my own life.

She asked me—and I did my best to answer her with recommendations about therapy and antidepressants, which had helped me. But it made me enormously uncomfortable, talking about my own depressions in a matter-of-fact way, as if it were just another blameless physical illness, like breast cancer. Intellectually, I knew that was true; emotionally, I felt differently.

It's easy for me to talk about my experiences with breast cancer. But I've rarely talked about my depressions, which have caused me the greatest and most crippling pain in my life. By doing this, I'm reflecting and accepting the culture in ways that make me ashamed of my own cowardice.

But think about it. When you're diagnosed with breast cancer, you have a disease that can be "seen" on pathology slides, so clearly physical that surgeons use their tools to cut at it. You are brave; you know this because everyone tells you how brave you are, even though you know you're only putting one foot in front of the other. Your friends—and you have so many of them, you realize gratefully—send cards and big bouquets of flowers, and they bring casseroles and desserts by your house. They all want to help.

But depression? You're trapped inside yourself, shrouded in darkness and hopelessness and relentless suffering. You wonder if you can survive the agony and torture of the next few minutes, the rest of the day. Do you see the problem? I use words like agony and torture because they're as close as I can come to describing what depression is like. But they're not close enough, not strong and graphic enough. They can't make you understand the torment of depression unless you've been there yourself.

Depression is a private hell. Those who have been there don't want to talk about it, and even if they did, the world doesn't want to listen. Nobody brings flowers or casseroles, and nobody tells you you're brave—even though the same act of putting one foot in front of the other is as brave as I've ever been in my life. There aren't any races for the cure, no ribbons or T-shirts for survivors to wear. This is a disease of silence and, at most, hushed voices and averted eyes.

But that didn't happen at the funeral for my friend's son. At the parents' insistence, both the minister and a friend who spoke made this young man come alive—his intelligence, his irreverence, his drive and humor—and their voices were loud and clear. They made you understand how dearly this boy was loved and how hard he and everyone who cared about him had struggled against his depression. But in the end, the therapy, the medication, and the love hadn't been enough, and the pain was too great for him to bear.

He had so much to live for, but still, he killed himself. Can you imagine how enormous his suffering must have been? If you've ever been deeply depressed, you can imagine it all too easily.

I watched my friend and her husband and their older son, their faces wrenched by grief. They want so much for some kind of understanding and compassion to come out of their great loss. Quietly and insistently, like the unanswered phone, they're asking for something. This is all I can do—to be honest about my own life and to try to make you understand. My silence has to end.

Rest in peace, Chase Walter Keller—you and everyone who loved you.

———————— 🍎 ————————

Spring Stories

Like everyone else in the bleachers, we went to the baseball game for different reasons.

I was there because it was spring break, and I couldn't get any work done. No wonder. There were four adolescents sprawled in the living room next to my office, inhaling soft drinks, cackling, and making fun of the horror movie they were watching.

Wouldn't a baseball game be healthier than that? I'd always wanted to take my son to a University of Texas baseball game, anyway. That was one of those things I'd filed in some kind of "remember to do someday" list in my mind. Besides, it was a beautiful spring day.

I gave the kids strict instructions that they all had to bring baseball gloves so they could catch any balls that came our way. If I got clobbered by a line drive, I hinted ominously, I'd quickly lose my good humor and immediately cut off my son's supply of junk food.

The kids came back to our house with money and baseball gloves and piled into the car—my son and his friends Skylerr, J.J., and Lee. Lee's a year or two younger than the other kids, with a sweet face and big, brown eyes. Earlier that morning he'd gone to see his grandmother in the hospital. She was a charming, vibrant woman—the kind of grandmother every child should have—who took the neighborhood kids to parties, miniature golf, and amusement arcades. Three weeks earlier she'd checked into the hospital for a routine hysterectomy and had never returned home. She'd been diagnosed with advanced ovarian cancer.

"It was hard for Lee to see her—the way she's changed," Lee's mother, Pam, said when I called her. "I'd seen her every day, and I guess I just didn't realize how much she'd changed."

But that afternoon, we didn't have to think about all of that. We could go to the baseball game. The kids spilled out of the car, laughing at some of the worst jokes I've ever heard, elbowing one another and racing to stand in line at the box office. I parked the car with my friend Martha, and we trekked back to the baseball stadium, winding our way through jammed parking lots and medians with shaggy new grass. The four kids were waiting in line by the time we got back, thumping their baseball gloves and almost vibrating with energy.

"I'm starving," my son said, since it had been at least an hour since his last meal.

We sat in the bleachers, close to first base, and the kids promptly forgot they were supposed to be protecting me from stray line drives. They leaned over the cyclone fence, right along the "Do Not Lean on This Fence" sign, and demolished several rounds of nachos, boxes of stale popcorn, and soft drinks the size of one of the smaller Great Lakes.

Martha and I sat in the bleachers and chatted idly about books we'd read, people we knew, and trips we'd taken. We talked about a lot of things. But what we didn't talk about was the checkup Martha had scheduled later in the week—the blood tests and CT scans to see whether her cancer was still in remission.

Instead, we talked about lots of other topics, and sometimes we even watched the game. The college guys who played were lean and good-looking as they stretched, heaved the ball, and dived for the bases. To look at them, so young and earnest, you'd think they were untouched by life's sadnesses and limitations. But maybe they weren't. Maybe that's a foolish assumption you make when you don't know anything at all about someone else's life.

We watched them play this game, where there were rules, predictability, clear definitions, and scoreboards. We had to leave before the end of the game, and maybe, I thought, that was just as well, since Texas was losing. We walked back into a world where spring was green and fragrant and where lives were ending and going forward.

It took us days till we understood more. We'd left before some kind of thrilling, late-inning rally by UT to win—the most exciting part of the game, and we'd missed it, Martha told me over the phone the next day. We were both irritated. How pathetic can you get, we asked each other, leaving a baseball game at exactly the wrong moment?

The days passed as spring break unwound like some sort of wild, chaotically colored kite string. The kids ran up and down the block and spent the night at each other's houses. Lee's grandmother died that week. The beautiful weather turned to rain, then back to brilliantly blue skies. Martha learned that she'd have to go to the hospital for a biopsy.

My son loved the baseball game so much, he says, that he wants to go back for his birthday. Why not? I think. It's his thirteenth birthday today, and we'll go wherever he wants to go. We'll go back to the baseball field. We'll watch the game if we feel like it. We'll wait for the final score and hope it delights us again this time. And whenever we get the chance, we'll lean on the fence or anything else that holds us up.

While we're there, we'll watch the clouds gather and pass and gather again. Spring is like that, you know.

Chapter 12

Confessions

Uprootings

Look at them.

They're drooping, as usual. They're also watching me reproachfully. They won't leave me alone, ever. I have green-and-yellow-and-brown nightmares about them.

"This plant is *angry*," my sister said when she was here in April. She pulled a potted plant out of the basket-holder it had been in. The roots were twisted, pushing out of the bottom.

This was definitely weird. My sister's usually a very sane person, I'd always thought, as long as you didn't count her obsessions with Eastern European countries, religious icons, and the occasional attack dog. She didn't normally go around talking about the emotional lives of potted plants.

But right now she was looking at me in what I felt was a very accusatory manner. I could tell she knew I'd never bothered to remember the official name of the plant she was brandishing like a dry, brown torch (because, if you want to know the truth, I didn't care to handle that kind of familiarity with something so low on the personality scale. It was a green something or other, that's all. Whatever.)

"It needs a bigger pot," my sister said bossily. "It also needs to be fertilized."

I nodded and tried to look interested and semi-responsible. But all I was thinking was, *Hey, do I look like a farmer? If the plant's that demanding, why don't we just dump it in the compost pit where it'll have a lot more room to decompose? Maybe it will be happier outside. I know I won't miss it.*

There. I've said it. I don't like plants in my house.

"What do you mean, you don't like plants?" my husband said, looking mildly horrified. "That's crazy. I think you're ambivalent about them. Or indifferent. That sounds better."

"I'm not indifferent," I said testily. "I hate plants."

What did he know? This man has never watered a plant in his life. No wonder he sounded so magnanimous. Not me. I'm sick of all the responsibility for those needy, green little flotsam that line my kitchen sink. They make goldfish look exciting, but they don't die nearly as quickly.

And I'd thought I was finished with them! We'd moved from Dallas to Austin three years ago, and at every possible juncture, left and right, backward and forward, I'd given plants away to friends. The 200-mile trip would be too hard for them, I'd hinted. I wouldn't want to take that risk. Better to leave them with someone who could care for them.

By the time we'd loaded up both cars, I'd managed to give away every green thing in our house. It was a getaway! Plant-free at last! We had each other; we had the kids and the cats. That was enough responsibility as far as I was concerned.

The weeks turned into months and years, and at every party and celebration at our new house, people brought plants. More and more plants. What were they thinking? Was this passive-aggressive or was it just my imagination? It was a jungle in here.

My friend Pat gave us a big Norwich pine for our living room. The minute I saw it, I felt ill. I knew that every time Pat came to our house, she'd be inspecting her present, and she'd track me down and kill me if it turned up dead. She'd never believe any excuses I'd come up with, either, such as how the pine was out of town visiting friends. No, Pat knew me too well.

In fact, I was pretty sure she knew my shameful history with plants and how they used to make me feel constantly guilty. Like the time I was interviewing some kind of freelance plant caretaker in Virginia and followed her through business atrium after business atrium, while she watered and spritzed and scooped and even talked to the big, green, glossy, healthy plants. After a while I was caught in a very big shame spiral about all the plants I'd killed over the years. I was still quite sensitive about the untimely demise of my late sheffelera after someone had watered it with a glass of vodka at one of our parties, even though my husband assured me the sheffelera had probably died happily in some kind of contented stupor.

But that was years ago. I'm over my guilt about plants. After having children, my deep reservoirs of guilt have been shifted and depleted in a human direction. I'm no longer deeply touched by little green things that don't have legs, don't follow me around, and don't talk back.

Not usually, anyway. But then the only plant I halfway liked—the aloe vera—just crashed over the side of its pot last week and landed in the sink, torn off at the roots. Was this a message? I wondered. A cry for help?

I would ask my sister, but I think I know what she'd say.

Celebrity Interviews Are So Unfair!

She's greedy. She's vile-tempered. She's a horrible mother. She used to scream at her (now ex-) husband and call him "that stupid Andy, that idiot." She went on a really strict diet and started working out, but she's still a size 12.

I know all of this about Martha Stewart because I've just read *Just Desserts*, her unauthorized biography. My first reaction was, *Hee, hee, hee, hee! I'm not a bit surprised! I always loathed Martha Stewart, anyway!*

But then I thought about it more. I reconsidered. I thought, *Uh-oh. Wait a minute. What if I become rich and famous someday, just like Martha Stewart, and somebody writes a really mean biography about me! A sleazy author could take events completely out of context—like the time I was five and I bit my cousin Elaine on the hand, for instance—and make it sound as vicious and unbalanced as Martha.* (Important biographical details: Elaine was messing with a picture on my bulletin board. She had to be stopped.)

That's why I agreed to answer this interviewer's questions. I wanted to come clean before someone decides to write my biography. I wanted to tell my side of the story first.

Q: So, let's skip the preliminaries. Tell me about the Thanksgiving dinner you cooked in 1972.

A: 1972? What? I can't remember what I—

Q: Oh, really? Well, let me refresh your memory. That was the year you fed two poor, unsuspecting Japanese students a greasy, half-frozen turkey with purple gravy—and acted as if that was the way all Americans cooked Thanksgiving dinner. Do the words "international incident" or "near-fatal food poisoning" mean anything to you?

A: I think my husband cooked that year. We decided I was better at cleaning up.

Q (sarcastically): I suppose that was after you started that fire in the oven while you were attempting to cook a steak for him?

A: That fire's always been exaggerated. It wasn't that big.

Q (under his breath): Sheeesh. Her husband must be a saint. (More loudly): You once were quoted as saying you were going to spray-paint the cobwebs in your house so they'd match your living-room furniture. Is that true?

A (weakly): Well, it was just a joke.

Q: Not a very good one, was it? But let's move on to your so-called parenting skills. Tell me about the cookie recipe you contributed to your daughter's kindergarten class cookbook in 1987.

A: I don't recall—

Q: You don't recall a lot of things, do you? Let me read you what you wrote: "Go to the grocery store. Buy a package of chocolate-chip cookies and take them home. Open the package as quickly as possible and place the cookies on one of your own plates. Take all the credit when someone tells you how good they are." (Menacingly): Does that sound familiar?

A: Well, I—

Q: And what about the time your son's fourth-grade class sent a little stuffed animal named Travel Bear home with him? All the good parents in the class took Travel Bear on trips with them and took pictures of him at places like the Statue of Liberty. But you didn't, did you? You went skiing and left Travel Bear, all by himself, in your car. You said that your bags were already full and that you didn't think Travel Bear would know the difference, anyway, since he didn't seem very smart.

A (eagerly, trying to make a comeback): Well, at least I didn't do what the father of my son's friend John did. (Note: This name has been changed to avoid potential lawsuits for libel. John's father knows who he is.) John's father took pictures of Travel Bear sitting on a hotel bed in San Francisco, surrounded by overflowing ashtrays and a bunch of empty beer cans. I think you should investigate John's father instead of me.

Q (shaking his head sadly): You disgust me. What do you think this is—the McCarthy era? (Clears his throat.) By the way, how many houseplants have you killed in your lifetime? One of your scheffleras swears it's in the triple digits.

A (garbled screams): This is outrageous! I'm sick and tired of being interviewed. Leave me alone!

Q: Just one more question. You see what I've got? (Holds up a legal document and smiles coldly.) It's an affidavit from your cousin Elaine.

————— ❦ —————

Good Neighbors and Bad

Ten years ago, I had a three-year-old daughter, I was pregnant with my son, and I had constant work deadlines to meet. Naturally, my husband was out of town the day my car broke down.

Our next-door neighbor, Ken, took me to pick up my daughter, who was at a daycare center about two miles away. On the way there, I'm sure I apologized to him every few blocks. This was such an imposition! He probably had lots of other, more important things he could be doing! It was so nice of him to take the time! I was sorry to be such a burden! Yak, yak, yak.

Finally, Ken stopped me in the nicest way possible. "You know, Ruth," he said, "this is the kind of thing a neighbor does."

That's one of those moments that I've saved, frozen and perfect. I've forgotten so many other things, important and unimportant, for those years. But I've always remembered being stopped speechless in that car, realizing that I'd been doing something very wrong.

I'd talked about how I loved living in an older neighborhood, with its mixture of elderly people, like Ken and his wife, who'd lived there for years, and younger families like our own. I'd talked about the importance of good neighbors and neighborliness, and what a wonderful thing it was to have a neighborhood right here, in the middle of a big city.

But really, all I'd done was talk about being a good neighbor. I was too busy with my life and my family's life to do much more than wave and roar off, at least when my car was running. I was moving too fast to take the time.

Busy-ness, I kept thinking. That was the problem. We were all too busy these days, with work, families, bills, music lessons, doctors' appointments, tax returns, and housework. But it was more than that.

We'd gotten used to constant motion in our lives. We'd forgotten what it was like to slow down, to take the time to be a good friend or a good neighbor. Human relationships came at their own slow, unpredictable pace; they weren't something you could schedule or mark off on a to-do list.

In the years since, my life has slowed some. I look back at my earlier self as too driven and hyperactive. Maybe it has everything to do with the fact that I'm no longer twenty-five, or even thirty-five, but I also like to think that I've lost my faith in constantly being busy and preoccupied. I like to think I'm using my time in more important ways, such as being a good friend and neighbor.

But then I watched recently as a moving van parked outside the home of an elderly woman who lives on our block. I stopped to talk to the woman's daughter and learned that she'd been in a nursing home in the East since the summer. I stood there and thought of our neighbor, realizing we'd probably never see her again.

Three years before, our whole neighborhood had gathered for her ninetieth birthday party. She was still beautiful, with a fine-boned face and lively eyes. I'd wished her many more happy birthdays. "Oh, honey," she'd said, shaking her head. "I hope I won't have many more."

How many times had I passed her house since then, thinking I should stop? It would be nice, I'd told myself, to stop in with my children to see her. She lived by herself, and she was probably lonely.

But I hadn't stopped. I'd kept on walking, and I'm sure I'd had other, important places to go to, even if I can't remember what they were. They must have been important, or I wouldn't have kept on walking, would I?

Ten years ago I thought I'd learned something about being a good neighbor. I wasn't as overwhelmed and busy now, and I thought that, surely, I'd become a better person. But I hadn't. When I'd had the choice, I just kept moving, because I had other places to go.

Whose Pain Are You Feeling?

Oh, brother. First, it was Gloria Steinem who said she identified—strongly!—with Linda Tripp. Women are always judged by their bodies, Steinem said, which is why poor Linda had been the subject of so many (unfair! mean!) fat jokes. Then Calista Flockhart, of all people, piped up and said she, too, identified with Linda, blah, blah, blah, something about being branded an anorexic, blah, blah.

All of which sounds very sweet and understanding, but let's get real. We're talking about Linda Tripp here, remember? I happen to think Tripp is much better off hearing comments about her body (flawed, but whose isn't?) than about her personality (Machiavellian, two-timing, and vicious are only a few of the many, many unflattering words that come to mind). I don't feel Tripp's pain the way Steinem and Flockhart appear to; she can feel it herself, as far as I'm concerned.

I realize, of course, that this isn't a very enlightened attitude. Everybody seems to be feeling everybody else's pain these days, and the truth is, it's getting kind of confusing. Whose pain is it, anyway? Is there some universal reservoir of human agony that we can all delve into? Watch Barbara Walters conducting any of her celebrity interviews, and she appears to be in tremendous pain herself (brows furrowed, mouth pursed) even before the interviewee breaks down in the required deluge of tears.

Bill Clinton, who felt everybody's pain, among other things, is an obvious example of pseudo-empathy run amok. So is the New York murder suspect who approached the mother of the girl killed twenty years ago and reportedly told her, "I feel your pain—but you've got the wrong guy." (What does he mean, *he feels her pain*? I think this woman deserves a Nobel for not popping him one, right there in the middle of the courtroom.)

I know, I know. In theory and assuming the best of intentions and clearest of consciences, it's a very appealing notion to think we can feel others' pain. It's wonderful and comforting to believe that we're all one, that we can share our deepest emotions. There's a big difference, too, I realize, between the fatuousness of weighing in on Linda Tripp's angst about her bathroom scales and trying, very honestly, to understand another person's most profound torments and fears.

But. But we're trapped within ourselves, in different bodies, different lives, different nervous systems, different zip codes, different cultures. There's something tremendously presumptuous when you tell another person you know exactly what he's going through and that you feel it as keenly as he does. Unless you've been through exactly the same circumstances, you probably don't know the extent of his pain; unless you're inside his skin, you don't know how well or poorly he's tolerating it. (Are you feeling my pain? Are you sure? You might just have a stomachache.)

Or maybe I'm simply talking about my own frustrations with life. If I can feel someone else's pain, then I can share it, divide it, conquer it. I don't have to confront my own helplessness—and everyone else's—in the face of randomness and tragedy. Maybe I want to feel others' pain so that life will be more fair and tolerable. Perhaps that's a normal emotion at a time when there's so much pain around that it seems to have become a national sport on TV, complete with flying chairs, brawls, bared teeth, and screaming fits.

It's easier to try to feel Linda Tripp's pain than to try to comprehend the stories that came out of Mozambique, where floodwaters swept away entire villages. After all, Linda Tripp can be fixed, presumably, with plastic surgery, feminist solidarity, and a heart transplant (listen, this woman *needs* one of those things); it's too late for so many others.

Maybe. But I'm still not wasting my empathy on Linda Tripp and her ilk. I do what I can for people who are close to me. I do what I can, and I'm well aware of how little it is.

I talk to a friend who's sick and probably won't get better, and I tell her how much her life has meant and what a good friend she's been to me, how she's an example of how I want to live my life. Right now, she's somewhere else, living on another plane that none of us can quite reach. I can't feel her pain any longer, and probably I never could. I'm just feeling my own.

I'm So Glad You Asked

What's been going on in your life?

I once made the mistake of asking a woman that at a cocktail party. Her eyes lit up like a couple of crossed wires, shooting sparks everywhere.

She was busy, so busy, she told me again and again. Her whole family was busy, scheduled to the max. Her son had piano lessons Mondays and Wednesdays, private soccer lessons on Tuesdays, soccer practices on Thursdays and Fridays, games on the weekends. Her daughter had acting lessons on Wednesdays, guitar lessons on Tuesdays—no, wait! That was Thursdays—and athletic competitions all the other days. She drove them everywhere, north to south and all points in between. She also worked for her husband, and he was busy, too. Go, go, go—that's all they did. They never stopped.

Ten minutes later, or maybe it was ten hours, I knew her whole schedule, day by day, commute by commute, lesson by lesson, but that wasn't the point. The point was, I knew I was supposed to feel impressed by all her activities and busy-ness, but all I could feel was a severe facial twitch coming on, along with a raging desire to be propped in the corner with a stiff drink.

We're so busy! It's a mantra these days that fills in all the blanks. If you're busy, you're important. If you're busy, you have a full life. If you're busy, your life has meaning.

I used to be busier myself, when my children were younger (and so, I notice, was I) and I had a full-time job outside of the house and my husband was traveling. I had scores of activities that were important, even if I can't quite remember what they were. I didn't have time for a lot of things, such as friends and neighbors and long, slow afternoons, even when the spring sun was warm and the flowers were blooming.

That's one of the wonderful things about being busy, though. You don't have time to think. You don't have to give yourself over to the pure unwieldiness and chaos of life. If it's not on your schedule, if it's not worthy of an appointment, you miss it. You're too busy trying to control life to live it.

But now I'm at a different age, and all I want to do is to slow down. That's what I tell everyone I know. I want to slow down.

I've finished a book, which is my usual signal to start another one—immediately. I haven't, though. Instead, I'm cleaning my house, room by room. Unloading drawers, rearranging photographs and pots and pans, piling up shifting mountains of clothes to give away, ransacking closets, pitching out old bank statements and expired warranties and recipes I'll never try, filling white plastic garbage bags to the top. My husband and teenage children cringe in horror when I tell them this, because I have the (undeserved) reputation as a loose cannon when I clean house, capable of throwing out airline tickets, family heirlooms, and other assorted treasures. They think I'm dangerous.

"They don't understand what I'm doing," I complain to my friend Cindy.

"Of course not," she says. "But go ahead and do it anyway."

We nod at each other and exchange one of those you-know-how-husbands-and-children-are glances. Cindy knows what I'm talking about.

But wait a minute. What do I mean, *they* don't understand what I'm doing? The truth is, *I* don't understand it either.

On the surface, I'm trying to simplify and quiet my life, straining to slow down and heave out the inessentials, purify, streamline, cleanse.

Beneath the surface, I'm not so sure. Maybe there are times in life, I tell myself, when you forge ahead, optimistic and surefooted, confident of the future, over-scheduling the present, and crossing off the past like a completed to-do list.

And maybe there are other times when you simply sit still and dig deeper, trying to find something there, even if you don't know what it is. That's what I'm doing now, I like to think. Going deeper. Looking for something.

While I clean, though, I begin to wonder if this is just the same busy-ness I like to complain about. Am I trying to discover something or obscure it? Does all this activity have anything to do with my close friends who are seriously ill and our daughter's going off to college in the fall? Does it have anything to do with this dark grief that seeps in when I stop too long?

What am I doing these days? I'm glad you asked. I'm cleaning the living room Tuesday, the kitchen on Wednesday, the den on Thursday, and other rooms next week. Go, go, go—you know how it is. Scheduled to the max, controlling everything I can control, busier than I've ever been.

In Praise of Proper Punctuation

When I heard that someone had finally formed an Apostrophe Protection Society in England, the first person I thought about was my mother. She spent the last few years of her life bemoaning the absence of apostrophes in possessives (e.g., ladies room) and contractions (e.g., its okay with me).

Since Mother and I didn't agree about a lot of things, I always felt compelled to point out that I found it even more deeply offensive when apostrophes popped up gratuitously in places they were not needed. (Let me make myself clear: You don't need an apostrophe to form a plural, so cut it out right now.)

For a brief period of time, I even had a sweeping, all-encompassing theory about apostrophes—that there were a finite number of the wiggly little things in the world and they were simply being squeezed out of the right places and landing in the wrong ones. Then I got a headache and had to stop thinking in such slippery, global terms.

But anyway, now that there's a new club I can join, it makes me realize that people like me need to be protected along with the apostrophes. We are the kind of people who notice punctuation marks, who care about them, who have even been known to argue about them. Who cringe at misspellings. Who hyperventilate when we hear dead-on-arrival grammatical mistakes like, "Between you and I" or "Lay down on the floor."

Yes, I suppose you could call us old-fashioned and nit-picky, but we can't help ourselves. We have been doomed to notice—whether because of our reading, our fourth-grade teacher, our parents, or some kind of hereditary grammatical obsessiveness as blameless as blue eyes. If something is misspelled or misused, then all is not right with the world. It's tilted, and we want the balance back.

But do you think the rest of the world appreciates our attention to linguistic detail? Ha.

I can give you example after example of corrective remarks made solely in the desire to be helpful by a person of good intentions (that would be me), which have been rebuffed. For example, a couple of years ago, I thought the secretary for our son's soccer team might be interested to know that the banner she had just put up misspelled the team's name. In fact, I was about to launch into an explanation of the differences between what she was writing (Lightening—a process of great interest to cosmetic companies like Clairol and of considerably less interest to athletic teams) and what the team's name really was (Lightning). But by this time she'd already stalked off the field.

Similarly, a member of the Apostrophe Protection Society was quoted in *The New York Times* as having attempted to correct an apostrophe abuse in the menu of a nearby pub, but "was restrained" from doing anything by her husband. I know the feeling, believe me.

A few years ago, at our local video store, I was naïve enough to think that the clerks might appreciate knowing that Katharine Hepburn's name was misspelled in the title of one of their new sections. I pointed this out (very politely, I thought) and the teenage clerk stared back at me as if I were deranged. Worse, he seemed to indicate some kind of confusion and lack of interest about who, exactly, Katharine Hepburn was, which didn't improve my mood one bit.

But I let it slide for several weeks, thinking I would give the store a chance to correct its mistake. Time passed, and I brought the continuing, egregious misspelling to the attention of another teenage clerk. Once again I was greeted with similar nonchalance. The word "whatever," as I recall, seemed to come up. At that point, I could feel my husband's hand on my elbow, guiding me out of the store. He had been restraining me, he said later, because he'd been worried I was about to climb over the counter and commit some kind of violent felony.

So now you understand how hard it is for some of us. If you see me on the street, if you serve me or someone like me in your store, and one of us points out there is some kind of problem with your sign or your menu, just be patient with us, because we are doing our best in a blighted, imperfect world. Then correct the damned thing, won't you?

Chapter 13

Aging—But Forget About the "Gracefully" Part

This Is Liberation?

When I heard that middle-aged women like Joey Heatherton, Patti Davis, and Farrah Fawcett are now *Playboy* centerfolds, I became so demoralized that I practically had to be airlifted to the closest spa. It was exactly the way I felt when I read that—thanks to scientific breakthroughs—post-menopausal women can now become pregnant.

If this is so liberating, I kept thinking, *why does it make me feel so tense?*

I know, I know. It's supposed to be wonderful news that women can be considered sexy and vibrant even though they were born sometime before everyone on the face of the earth had a color television and a laptop computer. The trouble is, though, we're still supposed to fit into that same perky, youthful mold of perfection, unwrinkled, fresh-faced, and firmbodied.

In other words, this isn't about looking good for *your* age; this is about looking good for *your daughter's* age.

Which is why Joey Heatherton trained for thirty hours a week to prepare herself for a full-body comeback. And why former first daughter Patti Davis, who's in her forties, objected to "nasty little press reports" accusing her of being middle-aged. (Although age must be a very confusing concept to someone who spent most of her twenties and thirties in an adolescent rebellion against her parents.) No one seems to know what—if any—sacrifices Farrah Fawcett has made to continue to look like a gorgeous ingenue. But assuming life is fair, she must have a really horrible-looking portrait stuck in her attic.

In short, you have to be fabulously lucky with your genetic makeup if you're trying to look like a teenager and you're really forty-five. Or you have to be willing to spend a rapidly multiplying number of hours working out and a small fortune to be liposuctioned, tummy-tucked, chemically peeled, lifted, pared, and stitched back together.

I guess it isn't surprising that a generation known as baby boomers is going kicking and screaming into that good night. But wait a minute! Isn't this almost like returning to high school and high school values of beauty and perfection, except this time around, you get to have wrinkles instead of pimples? It reminds me of an occasional nightmare I have that I'm still in school and I haven't studied for an upcoming exam. I wake up, panicked, then I think, *Oh, that's right, I graduated from there years ago. I never have to go back again.*

Watching my own children hover around both adolescence and mirrors, I'm relieved I'm not their age. I don't miss the self-consciousness, the self-scrutiny, the self-absorption, or the obsessions about face and body. I also don't miss the endless pursuit of the right diet, exercise regimen, posture, makeup, haircut, and wardrobe that will turn you into Cindy Crawford or Jean Shrimpton, or whoever represents the current standards of beauty and perfection you're always failing to reach. I mean, who needs it?

In my forties, for the first time in my life, I've felt more relaxed and comfortable about myself and how I look. I have a more honest sense of yes, this is how I look—imperfect and not so young, but interesting and familiar and, somehow, all right. I don't have to worry anymore about not being beautiful or perfect.

The years pass and the body slows and changes. Aren't we missing something important when we're constantly battling nature and aging and time, continually striving to be thin, unlined, and eternally youthful? What's wrong with acknowledgment of those changes—along with the compensations of middle years, such as maturity and self-acceptance?

I think middle-aged centerfolds are fine. Just don't tell me that saying a middle-aged woman can be sexy as long as she doesn't look middle-aged is liberating to me or most other women in their forties and fifties. It's just another impossible standard that isn't worth the time or the energy or the money.

One way or another, we've all graduated from that place, you know. We don't have to go back there again.

Chains Around My Neck

Recently, my husband and I have been having conversations like this in loud restaurants:

Me: I really like this salsa!

Him: What do you mean, you've been to Boston? When was that?

Me: Huh? What's wrong with the salsa?

Him: I said Boston! It's the capital of Massachusetts! There's nothing wrong with it!

By this time we're practically screeching at each other. If our children are with us, they're mortified. They're usually diving under the table or circulating in the restaurant, trying to drum up some younger, quieter parents who will adopt them and empathize with their needs for much larger allowances.

Anyway, this is why I (loudly) applauded the news that President Clinton is getting hearing aids. I read all the newspaper articles about how it isn't rare for someone his age to be hard of hearing under certain circumstances. What is rare, the articles said, is for someone his age to admit to hearing problems and do something about them.

That's when I made up my mind. If the president can admit his midlife frailties and take action, so can I. I'm not talking about my hearing, which isn't nearly as bad as my husband's, if you want to know the truth. (Besides, unlike the president, I don't have four-star generals sidling up to tell me great new ideas about starting a war. I think you should have extremely good hearing when you're making decisions about nuclear weapons.)

I'm talking about my eyesight. The minute I turned forty, all the fine print in my life became a great big blob. I ignored it for a while. But one day my husband and I were at a restaurant, which, if you've noticed a pattern, is where we seem to have most of the crises of our adult lives. The waitress brought us fortune cookies, and I couldn't read my fortune. My husband grabbed it and claimed it said: *You are blind as a bat. You need reading glasses.*

I can take a hint. After that, I got reading glasses. Lots of reading glasses. I put them on, I take them off. I take them off, I lose them. I lose them, I buy more. I should invest in eyewear companies. I should own one already. I'm pretty sure I have reading glasses in every room in our house, so why can't I find them when I need them?

"Why don't you wear your glasses all the time?" my husband wants to know. It's one of those sneaky, logical questions that I hate. He never notices his personal appearance, and he doesn't have the same deep pockets of vanity I do. Because I don't want to, I say testily.

"Why don't you wear contacts?" a friend asks.

That's a problem, too. I decide not to tell her that I have a minor phobia about having anything touch my eyes. The last time I went to an ophthalmologist and someone blasted a puff of air right into my eye (which, I happen to think, is a very sadistic and dangerous procedure, by the way) I levitated several feet into the air. I know this because one of my husband's colleagues was sitting behind me in the waiting room. "You should have seen her jump!" he told my husband, which they both seemed to find extremely hilarious. (The next time I see an ophthalmologist, I'm going to another state. That way, at least I can have some privacy.)

"Why don't you wear a neck chain for your glasses?" someone else asks. "If you do that, you won't lose them all the time.

The minute I hear that, I can feel my fever blister making a major comeback. I begin to mentally shriek: *Not me! Not a neck chain for my reading glasses! I'm too young for that! You must have me confused with someone old!*

Then I calm down. Why not? I think. Why don't I get a neck chain for my reading glasses?

"You've got to be kidding," says another friend. She's a few years older than I am, and she looks aghast. The way she's carrying on, you'd think I'm about to call a press conference so I can announce I used to baby-sit for the Gabor sisters. "A neck chain adds ten years to your age," she says sternly. "*Minimum* ten years."

Which is why I'm buying an avant-garde neck chain of brightly painted beads for my reading glasses. If I'm going to add ten years to my age, they might as well be neon, in your face, unmistakable, and flashy.

Me: So, do you like my new neck chain?

Him: No, I want moo-shu pork. We got chicken the last time.

———— 🍎 ————

My Hollywood Career Is Over

Last month I celebrated one of those in-between birthdays that everyone yawns about. You know, too young for Social Security, too old for liquor store clerks to ask for your ID. When my husband and children sang "Happy Birthday!" to me, two thoughts crossed my mind:

First, I thought, *Good grief, no one in this family can carry a tune*.

Then, I thought, *Well, I guess I never will have an acting career in Hollywood. It's too late now.*

You see, I've been watching movies and TV shows, and I've come up with some conclusions I don't like. On screen, middle-aged men get older and middle-aged women evaporate. The men age, and the women get younger. A lot younger. Like Jack Nicholson and Michelle Pfeiffer. Nick Nolte and Julia Roberts. Woody Allen and Mira Sorvino, who's hardly old enough to be his—well, don't get me started on that one.

I can do math. When a woman's in her forties or fifties, her romantic lead needs to be thirty years older. So, if I go to Hollywood and become a movie actress at my age, the only men I could co-star with are dead. Maybe that's why you don't see that many middle-aged women in the entertainment world. There aren't enough elderly men with a pulse to co-star with them.

Take, for example, the recent reunion of the TV series *Dallas*. Bobby's wife, Pam, disappeared and no one seemed to notice—not even Bobby. I never liked Pam, but I think some-one should have mentioned her, anyway. Someone should have said, "Oh, I wonder what happened to Pam. You know, that syr-upy sweet one who made everybody gag. Remember her?"

Sue Ellen finally showed up, but J.R. was busy hanging around his female attorney, who looked like the star of some B-movie like *Law School Lolitas*. (Also, I don't know how they're teaching students to prepare for the bar these days, but, frankly, J.R.'s girlfriend needed some serious professional wardrobe advice. A three-piece suit doesn't consist of a jacket, skirt, and camisole.)

I know, I know. I'm getting carried away and irrational, and I'm forgetting all the wonderful advances women have made in the media, blah, blah, blah. After all, Barbra Streisand stars in movies and so does Susan Sarandon. Cher never seems to go away entirely. Most of all, *The First Wives' Club*—with its three fifty-year-old actresses—was a big hit. Maybe, I hear, things will get better. Maybe we'll see more middle-aged women in front of the camera. Maybe they'll be paired with men their own age or younger. Maybe you can ice-skate in hell. Maybe.

Let's hope. Because there's something sad and profoundly disturbing about looking up one day and realizing that you aren't seeing yourself—or anyone like you—reflected in the cultural mirror. You see mostly younger women, free of wrin-kles and cellulite and the experiences of a longer lifetime, staring back at you. You tell yourself, *Oh, well, it's only a movie*, but then you realize it's much more than that. You're being told something about how a culture values women who are no lon-ger young.

"When I get older, I'm going to date eighteen-year-olds," said my favorite clerk at my favorite coffee shop. It was the week after my birthday, and he caught me on a very bad day.

"That isn't funny," I snapped.

He said he was just kidding, and we both laughed. That's when I knew what I wanted for my next birthday—aside from better jokes.

More movies like *The First Wives' Club*.

More vibrant, strong female role models who are forty or seventy or a hundred.

More appreciation of women with the kind of wisdom you probably never develop before something starts to sag.

And more icing on my birthday cake.

Let'em Flap

I've had it with over-the-top resolutions about self-improvement and a brand-new me. Forget it. It's so ten years ago. Or maybe fifteen, if you like to count, which I don't.

At this time in my life, I'm into routine maintenance and emergency repairs. I'm pretty sure this is what Barbara Howar called "the age at which you should not wave good-bye at the beach."

But I like to think I've come to terms with all that. *I have evolved as a mature, spiritual person who is too enlightened to worry about the passage of years. I am Zen-like. I am calm. I am grounded.*

All of which is why I was so surprised when my friend Marian announced at lunch one day that she'd been interviewed by a prominent magazine and *had refused to give her age*. Marian is a very evolved, mature, spiritual, enlightened, Zen-like, calm, and grounded person, I kept thinking. What was up? Why had she refused to tell the interviewer how old she was?

"We live in a culture where women are considered dead in the water—useless—when they age," Marian says. She recounts the story a friend once told her of being involved in a job-screening, and how a male colleague had automatically rejected the resumes of all women over the age of forty. "I refuse to be stereotyped like that," she says.

At that point, I guess I should have realized that there was some kind of international movement afoot that—*naturally*—I hadn't been aware of. After all, Marian's one of those effortlessly trendy people who puts the geist into zeitgeist.

In fact, even our kids think Marian's cool, because she a) dresses youthfully; b) drives a sports car; c) is an artist and a vegetarian; and d) knows a lot about astrology. (Every time I start describing disasters in my life, such as lightning striking our next-door neighbors' house and frying all of our computers, or how my friend Stephanie was attacked by a marauding centipede right in the middle of the afternoon in the produce section of a local grocery store and had to be transported by ambulance to the hospital, Marian never looks surprised. She always nods very knowingly and tells me it makes sense, because my moon is in retrograde or Santa Barbara or something like that.)

So I guess I shouldn't have been shocked when, the next thing I knew, I read an article in *The New York Times* about young women in New York—I mean, really young women! Children, practically!—lying about their ages. The article ticked off the evidence: Thirtieth birthday soirees for women who had passed that particular marker a few years back. Several friends who jointly swore to change the year of their high school graduation to five years later.

"I'm going to say I'm twenty-one until I'm thirty," one told the *Times*. "What's the advantage of being older? Your health declines, your husband leaves you for another woman, and you can't find a job."

"As your age goes up," explained another, in case we hadn't all gotten the point, "your market value goes down, unlike real estate."

Well, maybe that was just some sort of New York phenomenon, I told myself. Then I opened a recent copy of *Mirabella* to see an article on what the magazine calls the Women's Fib Movement. A thirty-seven-year-old American woman who moved to Australia for a brief time became—voila!—only thirty-two. She found it somewhat disturbing, she wrote, to have to fabricate lie after lie. What musical groups had been important to her? What TV shows? What generation did she belong to? Five years don't make a generation, obviously, but they make—well, something, some kind of difference.

Who was she, anyway? At thirty-two, she was different from her thirty-seven-year-old self. "It was frustrating to forfeit these little pieces of history," she wrote, "all these bits of color that had made up the mosaic of my life so far."

I mention all of this to Marian, and she reminds me—a bit testily, I notice—that she hadn't lied about her age. She'd simply refused to give it out, and she didn't regret it, either. "I don't want to be stereotyped," she says again.

She has a point, I know, a painfully good point. But do we play along with the game with the cruel, ludicrous rules that, as women, we're less valuable as we age? (This isn't a society that's kind to its elderly of either sex, I realize. But don't tell me that women don't get it worse than men and earlier than men.) Or do we fight it? And if so, how? By trying to come up with new rules?

I don't know. But the next time I'm at the beach, I'm going to wave. Let 'em flap, I'll think. Who cares?

Chapter 14

Moving On

The Imperative Tense

All of us had different reasons for going to Spanish-language school in Costa Rica last summer. There were students and teachers like my husband who thought Spanish would be useful. People like me who simply liked foreign languages. And people like our children who'd been dragged along by their parents for some kind of summer self-improvement.

But Holly was a different case entirely. She was learning Spanish, she said, because she and her husband were adopting three Costa Rican girls.

Three sisters! My jaw dropped to the floor and stayed there for several hours, which didn't help my accent. Holly and her husband, who'd been married for several years, were going from being childless to being the parents of three girls, ages three, five, and eight. To me, it was like going from zero to sixty in a car you'd never driven before. (No, make that zero to sixty without a car.)

"Think of it!" I told my husband later. "Three children all at once!"

He and I were walking along with our own two children, who were arguing about lunch. I could hear screeches of "Pizza!" and "Shut up!" and "Don't hit me!" I wondered briefly when they'd begin to argue in Spanish and whether we should consider that progress. I also wondered how much more noise three children would make than two. I was pretty sure it was exponential.

The days passed, and we and our Spanish classmates struggled with past tenses and gerunds and participles. Holly was especially interested in learning the imperative and carefully wrote down commands such as "Don't touch that!" and "Be quiet now!" and "You need to go to bed!"

At the end of two weeks, Holly was finished with her classes and ready to move on. She was scheduled to pick up her three girls at the Costa Rican orphanage on Sunday night. A week later her husband would join them, and they would all return to their home in Massachusetts.

She spent her last childless weekend with us and another family at an isolated beach on the Pacific. During the day we walked along the water and waded and swam. That night—the last before Holly was to pick up her children—she and my husband and I talked for hours.

So what do you say to someone who's about to become a mother? My husband and I were dying to give Holly lots of advice, of course. But somehow we ended up joking about most of it. This time next year, we told her, she'd be spending half her time at the mall and the other half at McDonald's.

Sitting there, drinking and laughing, I thought about how we'd brought our first baby home from the hospital eleven years ago, and how much our lives had changed since then. That was a great, remarkable divide in our marriage, before children and after children, and sometimes I wondered about the people we'd once been.

We'd thought that parents molded children. Now we realized that children mold us, too. How could you tell someone else what it was like—how wonderful and terrifying and fun and tiring and teeth-clenching and exhilarating it could be— and how everything changes? How could you prepare someone for pierced ears and Nintendo and pre-teen hormones?

Well, you couldn't, of course. So we ended up toasting Holly, too many times probably.

Since then I've sometimes looked at the picture we took of Holly, her husband, and their three bright-eyed daughters standing in front of a church in Costa Rica. I think of how expectant and excited they looked, and how much they had before them.

Somehow, I'm sure they'll all be fine. The way I look at it, any woman who knows the imperative in two different languages can go from zero to sixty pretty damn fast.

The Time Capsule

My husband worries about immortality. I worry about next week.

So, naturally, it was my husband's idea to bury a time capsule in our backyard. He'd been thinking about it for months, he said, ever since we'd found shards of Indian pottery outside of Taos last summer.

"What are people going to find from our culture?" he asked. "Great works of art and buildings will be saved. But they don't really reflect our culture. We need to leave pieces of our daily lives behind. We need to let them know what our lives were like."

He wasn't really talking to himself. He was kind of talking to me. I was sitting in the kitchen, reading a book and watching him out of the corner of my eye. Finally, I gave up on the book and just watched my husband. Outside, he was digging a hole in the backyard. Inside, he was amassing a ragtag collection of what he was now calling "cultural artifacts."

An old camera. A clock we'd never liked. A Rangers cap. A can of cat food. A troll and Ninja Turtle figures. Coins, batteries, a phone book, newspapers, record albums by Elvis, the Rolling Stones, and Bob Dylan. Pictures of our family, house, and neighborhood.

All of these made a certain amount of sense. But why was he including okra seeds? "They might not have okra in another few centuries," he explained, sort of.

Anyway, all of this may sound odd to you. But my husband specializes in odd. Like most of his ideas, the time capsule started quietly and built into some kind of earsplitting crescendo.

Our neighbors began to come over with their own contributions of Mardi Gras beads, a hairnet and an old brush roller, antique bullets, and pictures of themselves. Our daughter wrote a letter about how she liked to roller-blade and why Tonya Harding was guilty.

Outside, the hole got bigger and we hadn't had so much excitement in our backyard since our cat got run over and we had to have a funeral for her.

Finally, on a cool Sunday evening, my husband, daughter, son, and I gathered to bury the time capsule. (Which was really an old beer cooler, if you want to get technical about it.)

Inside it, insulated with plastic, we'd left letters about ourselves and copies of the out-of-print books my husband and I had written. "Maybe they'll be re-released and they'll be best sellers in the future," he said.

We put the time capsule in the hole and shoveled fresh dirt on it, and my husband said he hoped no one would find it for at least 500 years. He continued to shovel the dirt, and I stood there and wondered what would happen, eventually, to the time capsule. For a few minutes, I forgot to worry about next week.

I thought about those ancient pottery shards we'd found at Taos, which had always touched me. I'd envisioned a people who'd scratched out a hard living from the earth but had still taken the time and effort to paint their pottery and make something beautiful in their lives.

Like those pottery shards, the meaning of what we'd left behind would depend on the person who found it—if anyone ever did. What would they see? Treasures? Trash?

Who knows? All I could understand was my own interpretation. We'd placed bits and pieces of our lives in that time capsule and now we'd buried it. We'd go on with our lives, and maybe someday we'd move away and forget that we'd left anything behind.

But here, a couple of feet underground, we'd left memories of a time when our lives were full and good, and the four of us were healthy and happy. I still didn't care that much about immortality, unlike my husband; I cared about what we had now. I wanted to hold on to it for as long as I could, but I realized that someday I'd have to let go.

A Car Pool of Boys

I knew these boys, of course.

For years I'd seen them on soccer fields and baseball diamonds, sprawling in the dirt and wrestling and crashing into each other. In fact, one of them was my son.

"Five fifth-grade boys," I said to my friend Maureen. It was August, and she'd called to ask if we wanted to join a car pool. "We're talking about driving a car pool with five ten-year-old boys in it? They're like a pack of wild hyenas when they're around each other. What are we—nuts?"

"That's what someone else said, too," Maureen said mildly. "I told her I'd rather drive a car pool with five boys this age than five girls. At least they aren't as mean to each other. Do you want to join?"

We joined. The first day of school, I peered into the Suburban that picked up our son, and all five boys looked so clean and well dressed and subdued that I hardly recognized them. After that, though, they relaxed quickly.

The first afternoon I drove the car pool home from school, it was like *Animal House* on wheels. Four of the boys arm-wrestled and tried to get each other into headlocks. The fifth sat in the back of the car and blasted "Louie, Louie" over and over on his trumpet.

"I'm beginning to question our sanity," I told my husband later.

Except. Except the school year wore on, and we all eased into a lively routine of backpacks and band instruments, good-natured insults and boasting about sports. Since I was a mother, I was almost invisible when I drove, and it was like joining a boys-only club every week. When I picked up the boys, I turned off the radio and eavesdropped shamelessly. I liked to think I raised eavesdropping to an art form.

Who was going with whom? Who had gotten in trouble that week? Who had homework? Whose team had won? Would Bryan and you-know-who get back together?

The weeks and months passed. One afternoon the skies poured rain, and two of the boys stood outside with their faces turned up and water streaming off their clothes. Another afternoon a group of older boys shouted nasty insults at them, and all the way home, the car pool plotted how to get revenge. Maybe they should beat them up. No, that wouldn't work—the older boys were way too big. Maybe they should report them to the vice principal and get them suspended. (Ha! That would show them!) Finally, they settled on drawing mustaches on the older boys' pictures in the school yearbook.

One night my son and I went to the gym, where I stopped to talk to Pamela, a friend with two adult sons. "I don't know why I feel so moved when I see your son," she told me. "But there's something about his age that makes me remember so many things about my own sons."

I recalled what she'd said when I drove the car pool the next day. It was my next-to-the-last time to drive for the school year. I watched the boys crowd into the car, shoving a little and slinging their backpacks in and poking each other. I thought about how driving a car pool is kind of like experiencing the saga of a school year in brief, loud, colorful snatches of talk and bravado and vulnerability.

Driving these five boys, I'd seen their slow and subtle changes as they neared adolescence. They talked more about girls now. They were more careful about combing their hair and slicking it down with mousse. Some of them had braces. Their bodies were lengthening, and their faces were changing. Something had passed, so quietly and gradually, that I'd hardly realized till it was gone.

I put the car into gear and gripped the steering wheel. As usual, I had to nag the boys to wear their seatbelts.

Heavenly Bodies

When our first child was born, I was pretty sure I had my life under control. After all, I had a theory about it, and I love theories. All my husband and I had to do, I reasoned, was to make this one, massive adjustment to having a newborn baby in our lives. We'd make this single, traumatic leap into parenthood. Then we'd settle in. Then we'd be fine.

The weeks and months passed, and I wised up. I got a new theory. Sometimes I got a new theory every week. By the time our daughter wobbled into toddlerhood and finger foods and the "No!" stage, I realized there wasn't any one, massive adjustment to parenthood. Instead, it was clear to me, having a child required a never-ending, relentless series of adjustments. It didn't seem fair. When we'd just gotten the hang of being the parents of a newborn, for example, our newborn had moved on, and we had to catch up. How can you rest on your laurels when they wilt this fast?

The years passed, and we had another baby. I think I wised up even more, but it was hard to tell. By then I was too tired to have theories. Those were the years when I'm fairly certain my husband and I never finished a conversation or even a sentence. Cheerios were permanently stuck to the ceiling, the floors were squishy, and someone was always banging a spoon on the high-chair tray or scaling the bookcases like they were Mount Everest. *Having a child is like installing a bowling alley in your brain*—my husband read that somewhere. I've forgotten who wrote it, but the author is a genius. For years he was quoted a lot more than Shakespeare around our house.

When we had the time, we measured ourselves on the back of the pantry door. We were recording how much they were growing, we told our children, and how much my husband and I were shrinking. When we had the energy, we got a baby-sitter and went out for the evening. Sometimes we were so exhausted we could hardly wait to come home and fall asleep on the couch. We'd drive around and debate how embarrassing it would be to come home before nine o'clock. How much pride did we have left, anyway?

More years passed, and our lives gradually grew calmer. We could take our eyes off the children for a few minutes without being terrified they'd torch the house or impale themselves on salad forks. Our children weren't as wild, and we weren't as frantic as we used to be.

That's when I finally had the time to come up with a new theory. Looking back, it seemed to me, when our children were quite young, my husband and I revolved around our house where the children were. We always knew where they were. We always knew who they were with. Even though our schedule was demanding and exhausting, we had some kind of control.

But then we passed into the years when our children were school age, and they came and went more independently. Playing in the neighborhood. Walking to nearby stores. Roller-blading. Going to sleepovers. The old model, the old theory, didn't fit any longer. My husband and I were the ones who were fixed and static, and our kids revolved around us in orbits that were getting bigger and bigger. We were needed—but not as much, not as often, not as constantly. Which was what we always said we wanted.

Last week one of those orbits just got bigger. Our daughter turned sixteen and got her full driver's license. Many of her friends drive, too. When she leaves the house, we say things like, "Always buckle your seatbelt," and "You can call us—anytime—if you ever need a ride home. *Anytime*. Have we told you that?"

She rolls her eyes and says, yes, we've told her all of that a hundred times. What do we think she is, a baby or an idiot? Don't we trust her? Well, yes, of course we do. So we try not to repeat ourselves again, and we hope we've told her everything she needs to know. But we're sure we've probably forgotten lots of things that are important.

Reaching this new time makes me think about theories that come and serve a purpose and then go. I think about marks on doors in houses we've left behind—and about orbits and spheres and heavenly bodies and moving beyond the limits of gravity.

I read that the universe is continuing to expand, and nobody has consulted me about it, but I guess it's fine. Based on my own life, I suspected as much. My latest theory, though, is that it may be happening a little too fast.

On the Market

Our house is spotless. The wood floors have been refinished, the carpet's been cleaned, the paint has been retouched. We've replanted grass at the far end of the backyard, where our son plays soccer, and we've planted bright flowers in ceramic pots on our porch. Everything is spruced up, streamlined, and resurfaced.

In fact, our house has never looked better. That's because we're getting ready to sell it.

"We wouldn't do this for ourselves, but we're doing it for someone else?" I ask my husband. "So we can sell it? I think our values are all screwed up."

He doesn't say anything. This is because he's too busy baking bread. My husband is convinced that the smell of baking bread makes people want to buy houses. He read that somewhere.

"Fresh flowers," another friend tells me. "That's what you need. I almost went broke buying fresh flowers when my house was on the market."

We buy fresh flowers, bake bread, and nag our kids about making their beds and cleaning up after themselves. It's kind of like living in a museum, except it smells like a bakery.

When we get one of those calls about a showing in five or ten minutes, we start barking orders at each other like deeply disturbed seals. *Straighten that towel in the bathroom! Clean up the cat food! Load the dishwasher! Aaaarrggghhh!* This isn't conducive to a calm family life. Not that we had a calm family life to begin with.

Somewhere along the way, it occurs to me that having your house on the market is every bit as bad as dating—and I always hated dating. You have to worry about appearances and pleasing other people instead of yourself, and there's an enormous potential for rejection. I know you aren't supposed to take rejection personally, but I take everything personally. Especially my house.

Then one day the house sells. I wander around it and look in every corner of every room. Everything looks warm, comfortable, and familiar. I now realize that selling was a very bad idea. A terrible idea! What were we thinking of? We must have been nuts to put this house—*our house*—on the market. I don't want to leave.

We've lived here for ten years, and I love this house and I love our neighborhood. We've lived here through hailstorms, ice pellets, heat waves, and grade school and middle school graduations. We were here while our kitchen was being remodeled, and we were here the day the contractor peeled the roof off our house so we could add on two new rooms. We looked up, saw the blue sky, and told our children it was kind of like camping out. We've been here through water-balloon fights, lunar eclipses, and orthodontia. Outside, we've seen a walnut tree grow from a twig into a tower of green. We even buried a time capsule and one of our deceased cats in the backyard.

Who's going to be the neighborhood historian if we don't stay? Who's going to remember the Fourth of July when my husband and some of the other neighborhood men exploded a pipe bomb and almost wiped out the neighborhood? Or the day I got into such a heated political argument with our neighbor that my husband was convinced Buddy was going to attack me with a rake? Or the afternoon a hackberry collapsed on the street and blocked traffic, and all the kids came out and roller-bladed up and down the block? Or the Halloween our son dressed up as a Republican and got more candy than any of the other kids?

We clean out, throw away, and sell some of our stuff at a garage sale. I tell my husband that, after this move, I am never, ever going to move anywhere else in my life. Forget it, buster. No way, Jose. Case closed, finished, kaput. In fact, if I didn't like the house we're moving to as much as I do, I wouldn't even think about leaving.

So, welcome to the house and neighborhood, Capp and Jonathan. You get to be the neighborhood historians now. I hope you have as much fun as we've had.

A Trip on Christmas Eve

We had plans on Christmas Eve. We were going to have dinner at our house, and it would be warm and casual, with good food and good company. We'd have a fire in the fireplace, and the lights on our Christmas tree would flicker on and off, spilling bright colors on the walls.

We planned that, but we were wrong. Late in the afternoon on Christmas Eve, a nurse called from the rest home in

Midland, where my mother is being cared for. The nurse said Mother's condition had worsened, and she didn't expect her to live through the night.

I talked to my father, who was staying with us for the holidays. For more than a year, Mother hadn't recognized any of us, and she probably wouldn't know if we were with her or not. But it seemed important that she wasn't by herself right now. Midland was more than 300 miles away, but if we drove quickly, we might get there in time.

My father and I threw our clothes in suitcases and quickly packed his car. We hugged my husband, daughter, and son, wished each other a Merry Christmas, and told them goodbye. Then we drove off into the pale winter twilight.

This wasn't the Christmas Eve I had planned or wanted, leaving my family and everything that was warm and comfortable in my life. But too often, I've noticed, you don't get what you want or plan for or think you need, anyway. Sometimes it seemed as if there was so much that was unpredictable and irrational in our lives that I wondered why we bothered to plan or why we kept trying so hard. But we kept on pushing and trying, and I wasn't sure why. Maybe because it was the only thing we knew how to do.

We drove over the winding roads outside Austin as the sunlight faded, the night grew darker, and the stars came out. In every small town we drove through, holiday lights were strung on the courthouses and town squares, blazing color and life and high spirits.

Gradually, as we drove farther into West Texas, the highway grew straight and flat. Around us, the traffic dwindled and the towns stretched farther apart. Between the towns, the road was lonely and the darkness loomed over us, vast and desolate. Occasional headlights from other cars appeared and disappeared, and the scattered towns were brief bursts of light. But mostly there was the darkness and an immense, lonely world that stretched in front of us, blank and all-encompassing and empty.

I switched on the radio, trying to find music. Daddy and I listened to Christmas carols and sang along with them. We'd always been the worst singers in our family, and we hadn't gotten any better with time. It was Mother who had the lovely voice that soared and my sister Ellen who had the good musical ear and played the violin beautifully. But Ellen was thousands of miles away right now, and Mother was lying in the nursing home where she'd been cared for more than a year. She'd been crippled by a rare neurological disease, and then she'd lost her mind and her awareness. So much of her had already gone that life and death had become technicalities.

I could hear Mother's voice the way it used to be, when she could still sing and play the piano. I thought about times we'd had that were good and bad, and times we'd laughed together. We'd never had an easy or a simple relationship, and nothing could change that. But she'd loved us, and she'd left Ellen and me with her sly, irrepressible sense of humor. She'd taught us how to laugh. I knew that, but I'd forgotten it. Sometimes you forget important things like that.

Daddy and I drove on through the black night, and we croaked out Christmas carols and sometimes we talked. But for the most part, we just sang. The miles passed and when we finally reached Midland, Mother's condition had stabilized. She was still dying, but she wasn't in immediate danger. My father and I stroked her hair and told her we loved her, but there wasn't much we could do. Before I left, I told her goodbye and hoped she would go soon, in peace.

And then I came back to my family to wait. That's the only thing you can do sometimes. You can't plan; you can only wait.

Ever since I've been back home, I've thought about Christmas Eve and our long drive through the West Texas prairies. It was a night when that huge darkness was such a real and immediate presence in my life that I could almost reach out and touch it. In that darkness and silence, I'd remembered things and heard voices that I never wanted to forget.

When I laughed or when I cried—but mostly when I laughed—I wanted to remember.

Music I'd Almost Forgotten

It was the usual garage sale, with a sign and arrow pointing to it.

Outside the garage, it had spilled onto the driveway. Sheets, towels, and blankets lined the tables, and drinking glasses and casserole dishes glistened in the sun. Dresses, jackets, and pants swung from the big metal hanging rack, close to the beige patio furniture. Paperback and hardback books over-flowed the cardboard boxes.

People came in pickup trucks and new sedans, unloading bright-eyed children and carrying babies in their arms. They leafed through the books and turned on the radio to see if it worked. With frowns on their faces, they carefully examined the bicycles, costume jewelry, and empty picture frames.

It was the usual garage sale you could see in any neighbor-hood in the spring, summer, or fall. But for me, it was different. Today we were selling the remnants of my parents' household. My mother had died a year and a half ago, and my father was moving to a studio apartment too small to house much furni-ture. It was time to sell objects they had accumulated during their fifty years together—things that no longer fit into my father's new life alone.

Things. Material *things.* They weren't supposed to be important, were they? Sitting out in the hot West Texas sun, they looked ordinary and undistinguished, just like the garage sale itself. But they had framed a lifetime. When I looked at them, scenes from my sister's and my childhoods and my parents' younger years unreeled like the music from the radio.

"How much is the piano?" a young, dark-haired woman asked. She pointed inside the garage, where the piano sat against the wall.

My brother-in-law Jim, who'd done all the work for the garage sale, was firm. Seven hundred dollars, he said. That's what he'd been told the piano was worth. He wouldn't come down to the $500 this woman was offering. No way.

"It's a good thing you're handling this—instead of me," I said to Jim after the woman had left without the piano. I'm the worst negotiator in the world, a shipwreck in the sea of commerce. Put me in charge of selling anything, and pretty soon, I'll be paying people to take it. Begging them.

"Leave it to me," Jim said.

I sat in the shadows of the garage and watched people ramble between the tables, touching things and looking at them more closely. A sense of melancholy poured over me, and I thought how forlorn all those things looked, stripped away from where they'd always been. I couldn't tell which upset me more—when people bought something that had belonged to my family or when they didn't buy anything at all. Didn't they know how important—how nice?—the objects were and the meanings they held? Of course they didn't.

But after a while, as the sun grew brighter and more relentless in the sky, I relaxed. There was something comforting, it occurred to me, about possessions being sifted and absorbed into others' lives. They were being carried away in boxes and sacks and by hand to new places and futures I couldn't see, reinvented and useful again.

As the hours went on, the cigar box of money bulged with wadded-up bills and people mopped their brows and complained about the heat. A truck pulled up, and the patio furniture was loaded into the back. Then the small dryer was hauled off to a nearby vehicle. The crowds dwindled in the hot sun.

For a couple of hours, I took my son to the bowling alley and watched him play. When I returned, the driveway was quiet and almost empty. I knew what I wanted to do.

I went inside the garage and sat down at the piano. Looking at it, I could remember how excited we'd all been the day we bought it almost forty years ago. I could see my mother sitting at it, playing and singing her favorite songs. More than anything, she'd loved music. She'd insisted that I take piano lessons, even after I'd lost all interest in the instrument. For five long years, I'd had strict piano teachers who had taught me well, even though I was a reluctant, sullen student.

I started to play what I could. My fingers were flaccid and weaker than they used to be, and I'd forgotten most of the pieces I used to know by heart. I picked out a few measures of a Beethoven sonata, then a Clementi sonatina. After so many years, I could remember only snatches of music, phrases that danced in and out of my mind before I could catch them. But I played what I could, still curving my wrist up in phrasing, the way I'd been taught.

Slowly and haltingly, the music spilled out. Maybe it sounded terrible, but I didn't care. I was playing the piano the best I could, touching it for the last time.